POISON ELVES
-VOLUME SIX-
Sanctuary
Books 3 & 4

Guild War & Strange Days
by drew hayes

POISON ELVES Trade Paperback Vol. 6. "Sanctuary" Part Two. June, 2000. FIRST PRINTING. Published by SIRIUS Entertainment, Inc. Lawrence Salamone, President. Robb Horan, Publisher. Joseph Linsner, Art Director. Mark Bellis, Managing Editor. Production by McNabb Studios. Poison Elves is © and TM 2000 Drew Hayes. SIRIUS & the DogStar logo are ® 2000 SIRIUS Entertainment, Inc. All rights reserved. Any similarity to persons living or dead is purely coincidental. Printed in the USA.

bow to the working man

longevity baby. longevity, guts and the balls to go the distance. that's what the man's got. who else can say that?

how many people in this spineless, fan boy-driven industry are willing to stick it out and keep putting their books out, month after month, year in and year out? huh? how many? who has the fierceness of vision? who has the sack to sit and do the work? not too many.

no, instead we have whipped creators working for the big corporations, whining about it like company x is their daddy, or worse yet, like they have no choice. or you got hot creator of the month doing two issues of a book, cashing his check and using the bucks to spank the monkey into obscurity while his readers and retailers say, "what the heck?".
or you got some work for hire guy selling his sob story about doing his own gig, telling his stories - someday. in essence, we have a putrid cesspool of lazy slackers, mindless excuses and forgotten dreams, of the whipped.

then you have the man. you know who i'm talking about. drew. the one and only. the author & cartoonist of this here tome, a tornado of unbridled storytelling energy. a pioneer. he's sitting there, doing his damn job and turning out poison elves. and he's up to issue #60 as of this writing. he's not talkin' about it, he's forcing his vision on the world. he's doing it. and we're buyin' it. issue after issue. year after year. forget trends. forget fads. bow to the working man.

if you ask me, in this world of the weak willed and spineless, the guy's a fuckin' national treasure. nuff said. now go read the books.

brian pulido
creator, chaos! comics

POISON ELVES
STARTING NOTE

Hello...

Up to this point in these Intros, I have catalogued my life and experiences in conjunction with the issues represented within the given volume. At this point, as this volume reprints the Sirius issues of POISON ELVES #13-25, I feel no more need to do this, as at that point in my career my "hands on" within the business itself had begun to and continued to grow into more of a social role instead of a business role. As I do not intend these Intros to turn into tales of drinking with the Chaos! Comics crew, or drooling over the Vampirella model with this or that artist, or tales of Danzig's con parties, I'd like to take the time to talk more of what the story within was about - what was behind it.

Although I have one, solid piece of advice for ANY comic artist/writer who busts ass for years and finally makes a name for themselves: if, at this point, you get involved with any women- DO NOT LET THEIR WORDS OF HOW GREAT YOU ARE GO TO YOUR HEAD!

You are still a peon artist in a biz of much better artists, the world CAN and WILL survive without your book, and ego makes you ugly.

I made the mistake, and I hate to admit this, of letting this happen for a brief time. Hey-it's great if your girlfriend thinks you're the shit, but don't trap that sunshine up your ass and shit it out on everyone else. Nothing is more pathetic than seeing that girlfriend-instilled ego-glow beaming off an artist while the neurotic little harpy keeps cawing on his shoulder.

Anyway.

SANCTUARY.

What the hell was I thinkin'?

Well, I knew I wanted to do a long, multi-issue story. I had "Sanctuary" planned before issue #1 of I, LUSIPHUR, but only roughly. I knew I wanted to tell a story about a secret organization of assassins, tell a bit of the differences between medieval crime detection and modern investigative techniques, and I wanted to blindly tell the first half of the story and see if I could tie it all up later.

I have this problem.

I've drawn all my life. So when I started doing comics, I saw writing as a necessary evil to draw them. I always figured I'd be respected most for my art.

Well, it didn't work that way. I'm generally considered a better writer than an artist. This is great, but was quite a surprise once I figured it out. But I LIKE being respected mostly for writing. I even surprised myself by being better than I thought I would be (not that I'm all Mr. Ego about it).

But in this, I developed a belief.

I remember in the first or second grade, the teacher would draw a line or a squiggle on the board, and we were to-one by one-come up and incorporate that line into a drawing. As for writing, I believe a good writer can lay down a group of incidences,

POISON ELVES
STARTING NOTE CONTINUED

set up some props, and eventually tie it all together, no matter how convoluted or messed-up things might seem.

My problem is, the ability to do this is what separates good writers from bad...

Or ONE thing that separates them, I should say.

So-I consider issues 1 through 24 of "Sanctuary" my squiggle. I figured out several definites I wanted set up, and winged it between them. The set-up of the "Sanctuary" itself, Vido and the Blood Guard, the relationship between Cassy and Luse (which I wish now I'd developed one issue at least more in-depth), Jace's involvement...

POISON ELVES is about a world going through a great change. The stories are about an elf, Luse, going through his own changes.

He is a character that, like it or not, came up from huge violence into great violence. The story centers on him because he is the one character in the book that goes through the most changes. The elf he was in #1 will be only a familiar stranger to who he becomes.

In "Sanctuary," he gains everything he thinks he ever wanted, but by the final installment of this volume, it begins to all get taken away.

Issue #25 is the first swing I took at deliberately ending the story. His trial was a set-up for this.

And for those of you eagerly awaiting Cassy's comeback, the next line is for you...

Ha-ha.

Repeat as necessary.

6.6.00
Ferndale, Washington

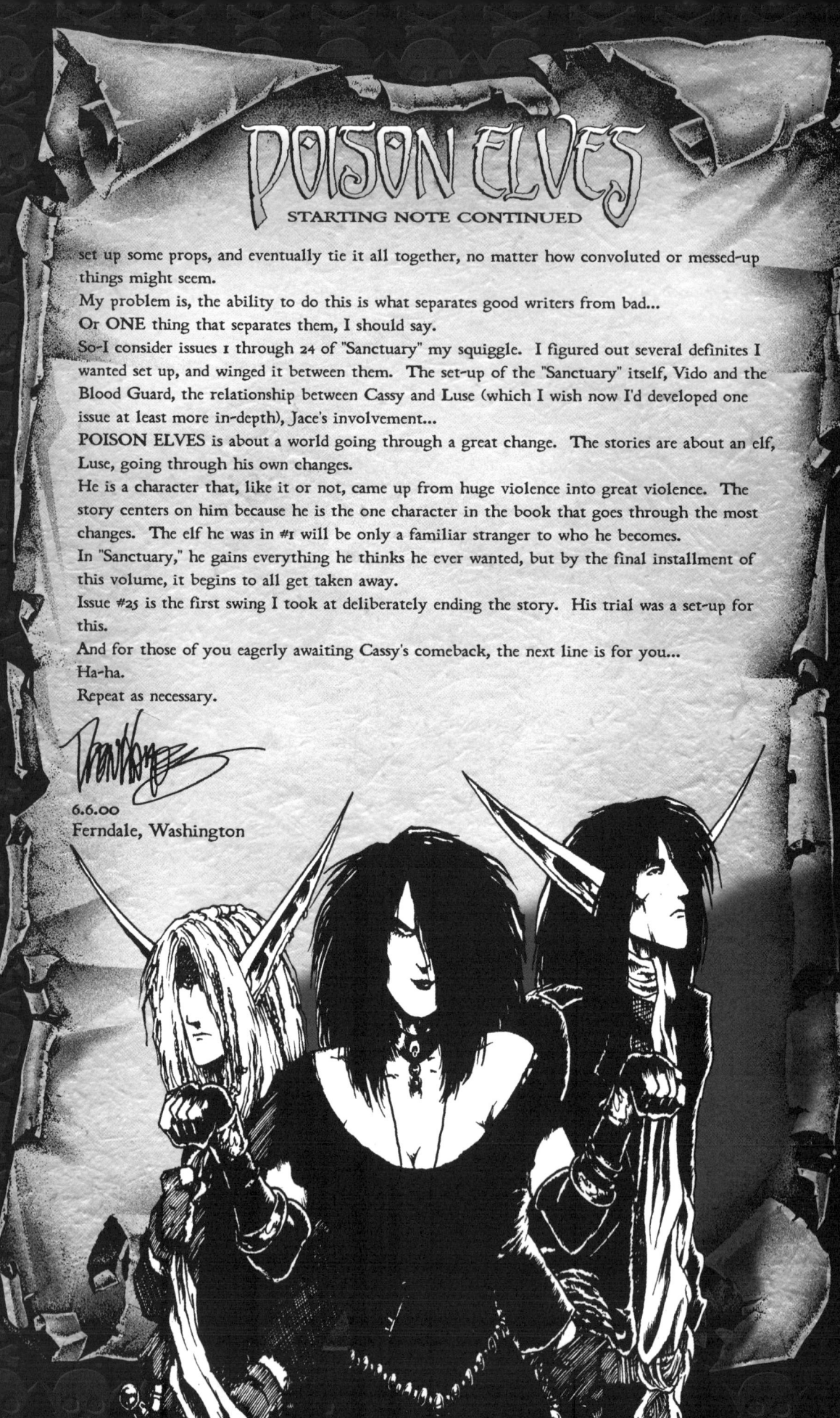

SANCTUARY

book three:

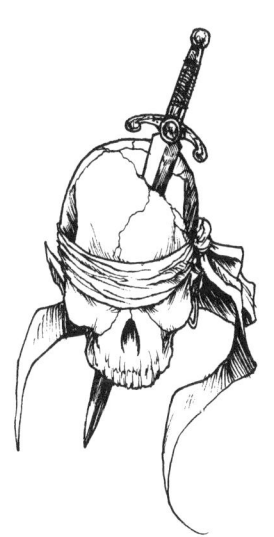

GUILD WAR

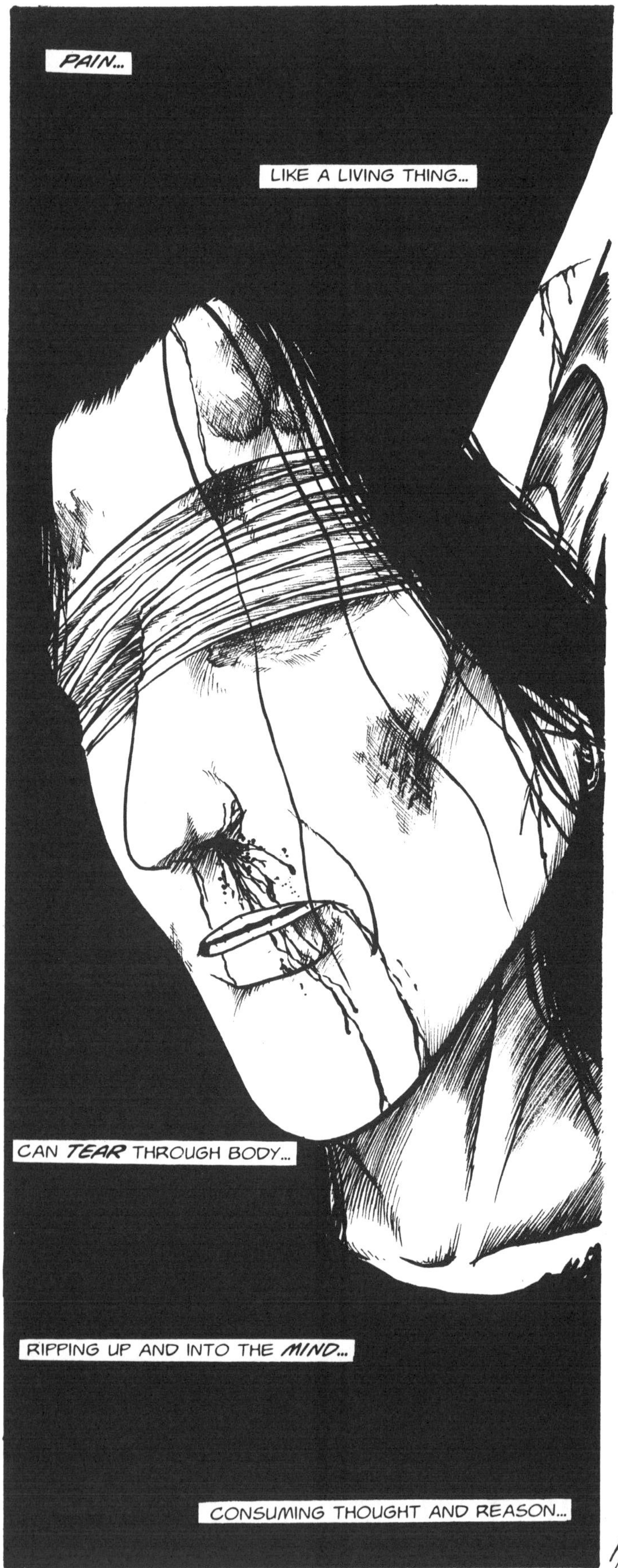

ONE

PAIN

PAIN...

LIKE A LIVING THING...

CAN *TEAR* THROUGH BODY...

RIPPING UP AND INTO THE *MIND*...

CONSUMING THOUGHT AND REASON...

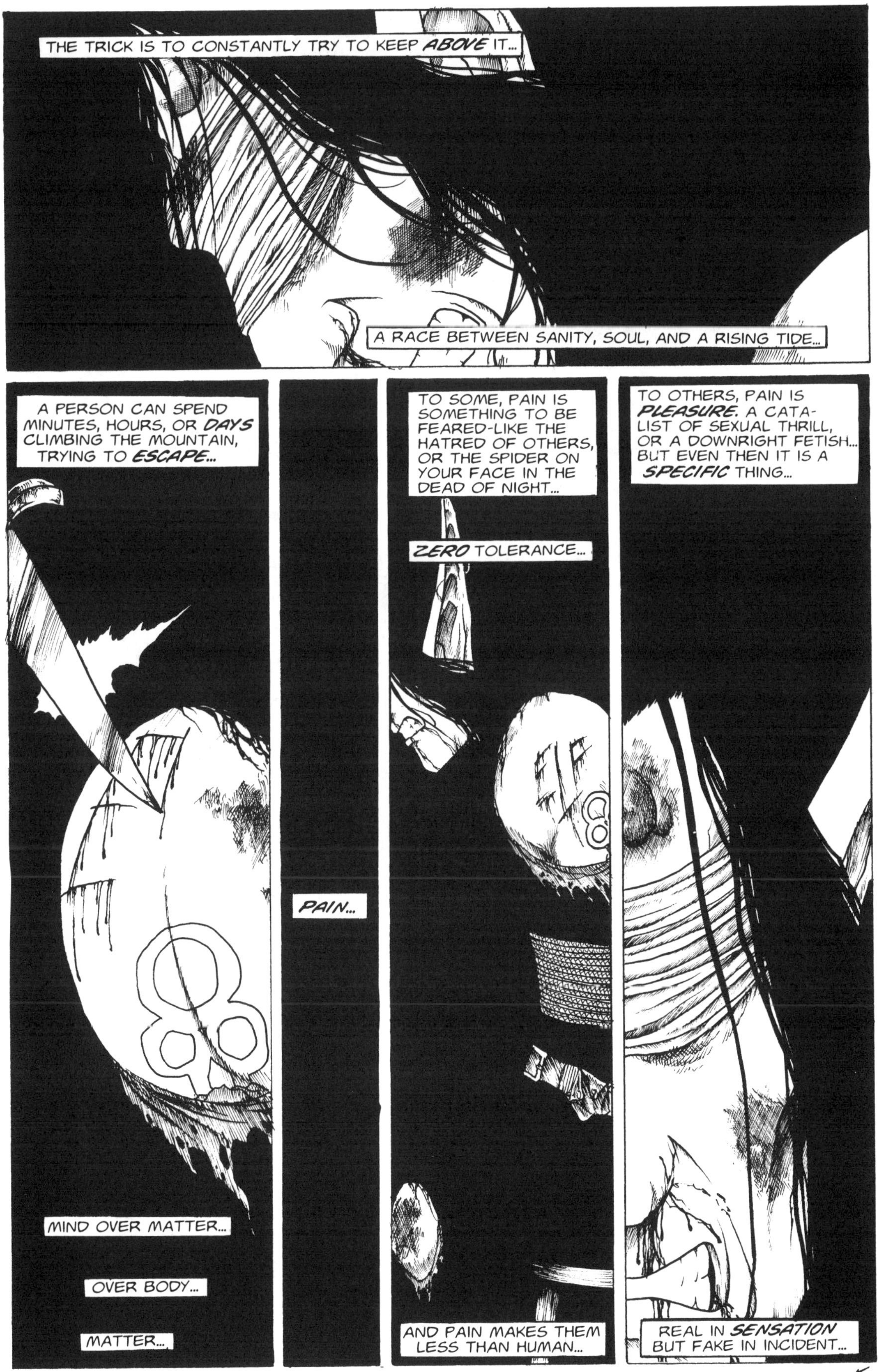

THE TRICK IS TO CONSTANTLY TRY TO KEEP *ABOVE* IT...

A RACE BETWEEN SANITY, SOUL, AND A RISING TIDE...

A PERSON CAN SPEND MINUTES, HOURS, OR *DAYS* CLIMBING THE MOUNTAIN, TRYING TO *ESCAPE*...

MIND OVER MATTER...

OVER BODY...

MATTER...

PAIN...

TO SOME, PAIN IS SOMETHING TO BE FEARED-LIKE THE HATRED OF OTHERS, OR THE SPIDER ON YOUR FACE IN THE DEAD OF NIGHT...

ZERO TOLERANCE...

AND PAIN MAKES THEM LESS THAN HUMAN...

TO OTHERS, PAIN IS *PLEASURE*. A CATALIST OF SEXUAL THRILL, OR A DOWNRIGHT FETISH... BUT EVEN THEN IT IS A *SPECIFIC* THING...

REAL IN *SENSATION* BUT FAKE IN INCIDENT...

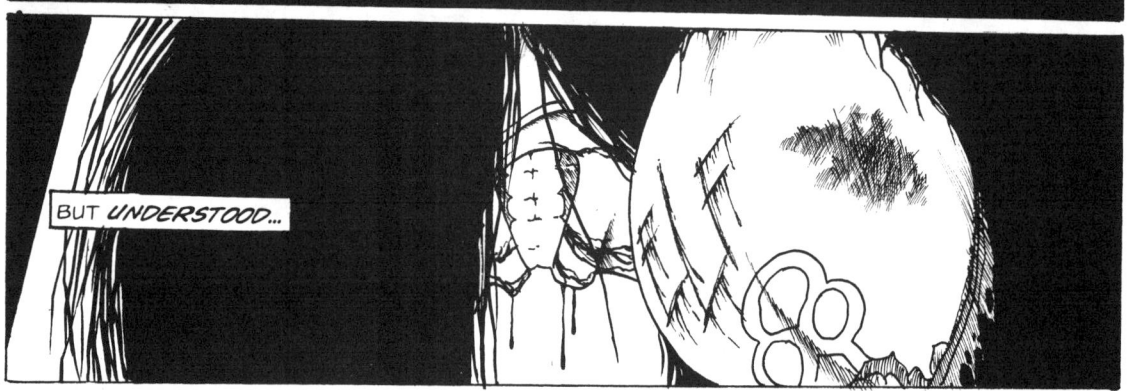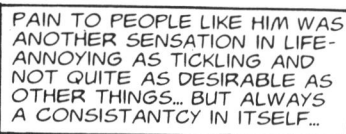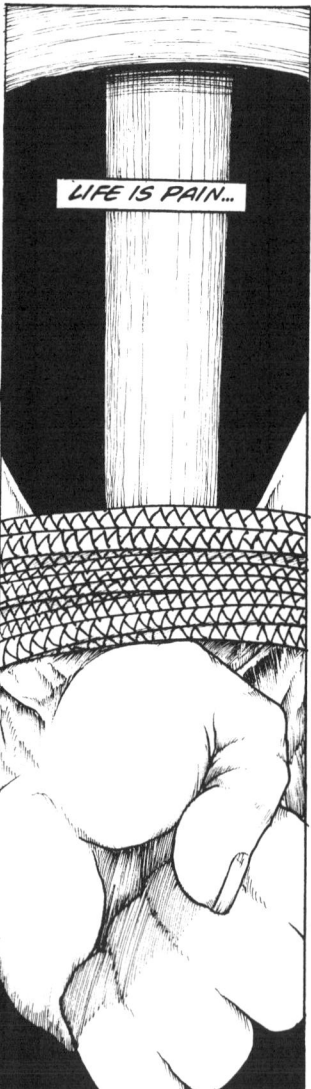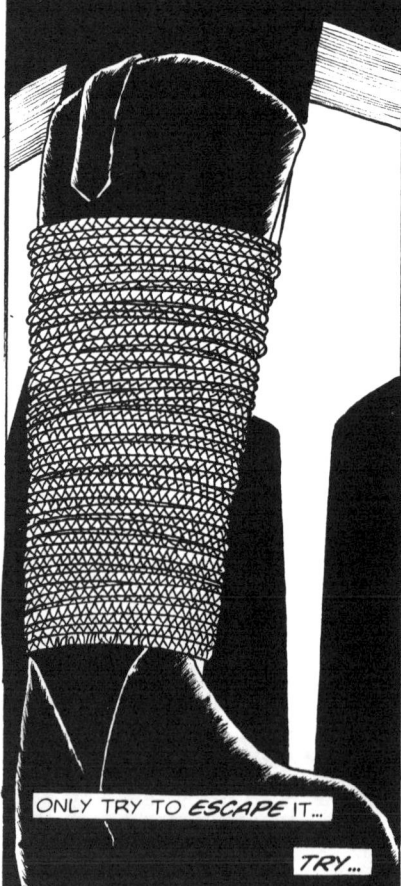

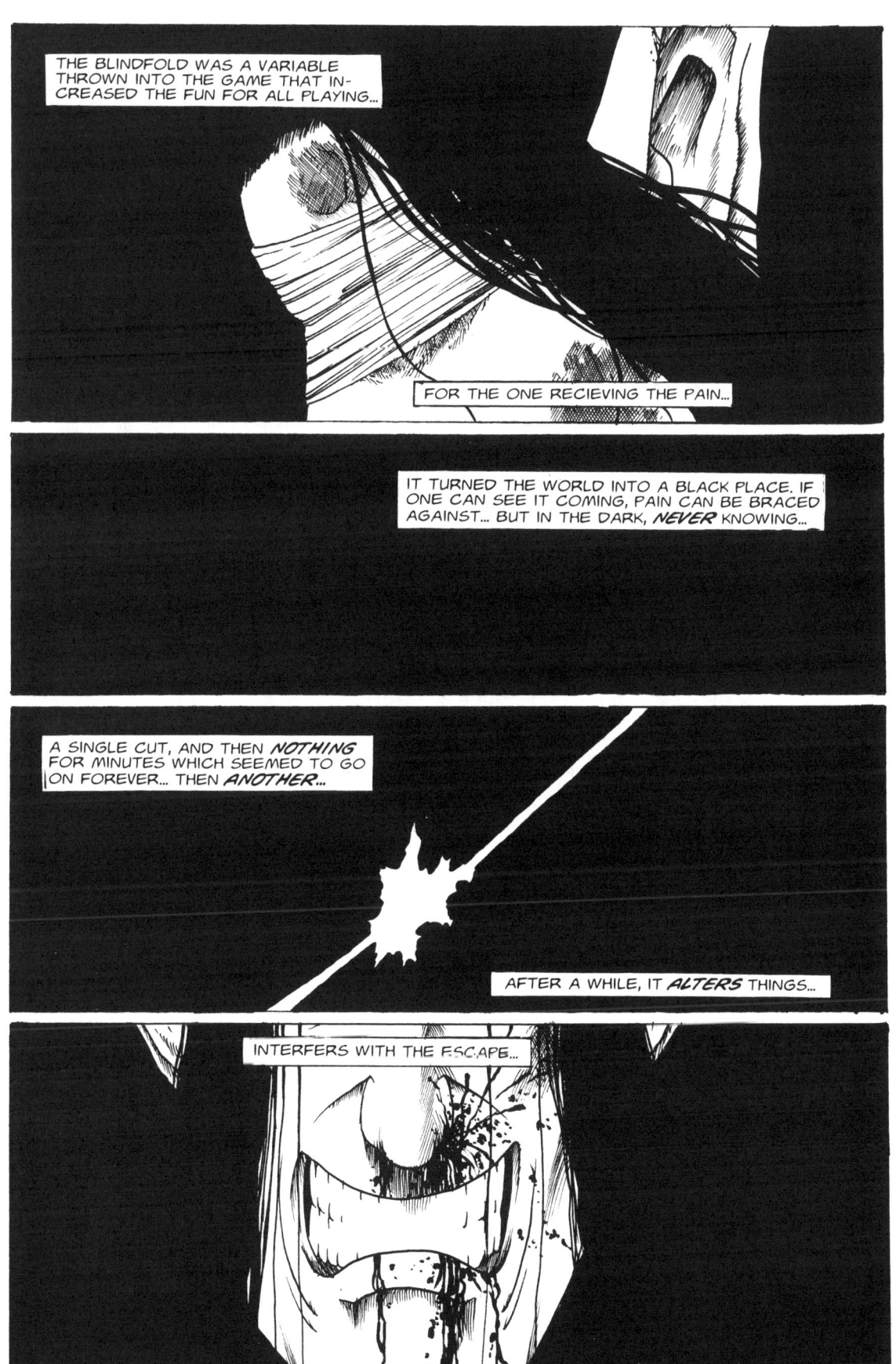

Mogre-Ur: So did you ride long to get here?

Morachi: I never ride anywhere- you know this...

Mogre-Ur: Hmmm... Yes. Were you seen?

Morachi: Was I announced?

Mogre-Ur: Actually, you broke into my chambermaid's linin closet and... Alright, you weren't seen...

Morachi: It's so nice to be such a welcome member of your little Elf club... I suppose this means the country estates are still off limits...

Mogre-Ur: Now, Morachi...

Morachi: And the swimming pools, and the saunas...

Mogre-Ur: You know your membership in the Council is invaluable, so stop this rubbish... Would you like a drink..?

Morachi: Sure. Hot wine with spice.

Mogre-Ur: Any word on your wife's mother?

Morachi: She's alive, living down south. 'Be down there another couple months...

Mogre-Ur: Miss her?

Morachi: Of course I do- she's my wife.

Mogre-Ur: Prehaps you should improve your aim, then... HAHHAHAHAH!

Morachi: Ohhh, you crafty Wizard types...

Mogre-Ur: I know, I know... A page told me that one yesterday- just about killed me...

Morachi: Oh, and to wonder why I don't live in a Step... Think of everything I'm missing...

Mogre-Ur: Morachi- if you lived in a Step, you'd probably be long dead...

Morachi: Moger, with yuks like that flyin' around I don't doubt it...
And despite all this, no- I was not seen by beast nor fowl... Last thing I need as well is any of MY pals finding out I'm here with you...

Mogre-Ur: Our pals certainly do not like eachother, do they...?

Morachi: No.

Mogre-Ur: Well then, come sit and tell me of what brings the great Thief King to First Step... I trust this has nothing to do with the Council itself or any of our "pals" in conflict...?

Morachi: Heh. Actually- it's got everything to do with that...

Mogre-Ur: Oh?

Morachi: But as you Wizards like to be so cryptic, I figure thieves can speak with forked tongues, so bear with me and you'll know everything soon enough...

Mogre-Ur: Alright...

Morachi: How's the investigation into Ailwon's death going...?

Mogre-Ur: ...Slowly. I find this a peculiar quest-

GRUFF LAUGHTER IS HEARD OCCASIONALLY AND LUSIPHUR KNEW AT LEAST FOUR MEN FILLED THE ROOM... TWO OF THE FOUR WERE THE ONES HURTING HIM...

VIDO'S MEN...

PAIN ON HIS HEELS LIKE A HELLHOUND...

CLAMP DOWN...

DUCK UNDER IT...

CLENCHED TEETH...

FISTS...

WHITE KNUCKLES.

SAY NOTHING...

THE KEY IS THE KNOWLEDGE THAT...

YOU CAN'T ESCAPE FOREVER...

AND THEN...

QUESTIONS PIERCE THE FOG...

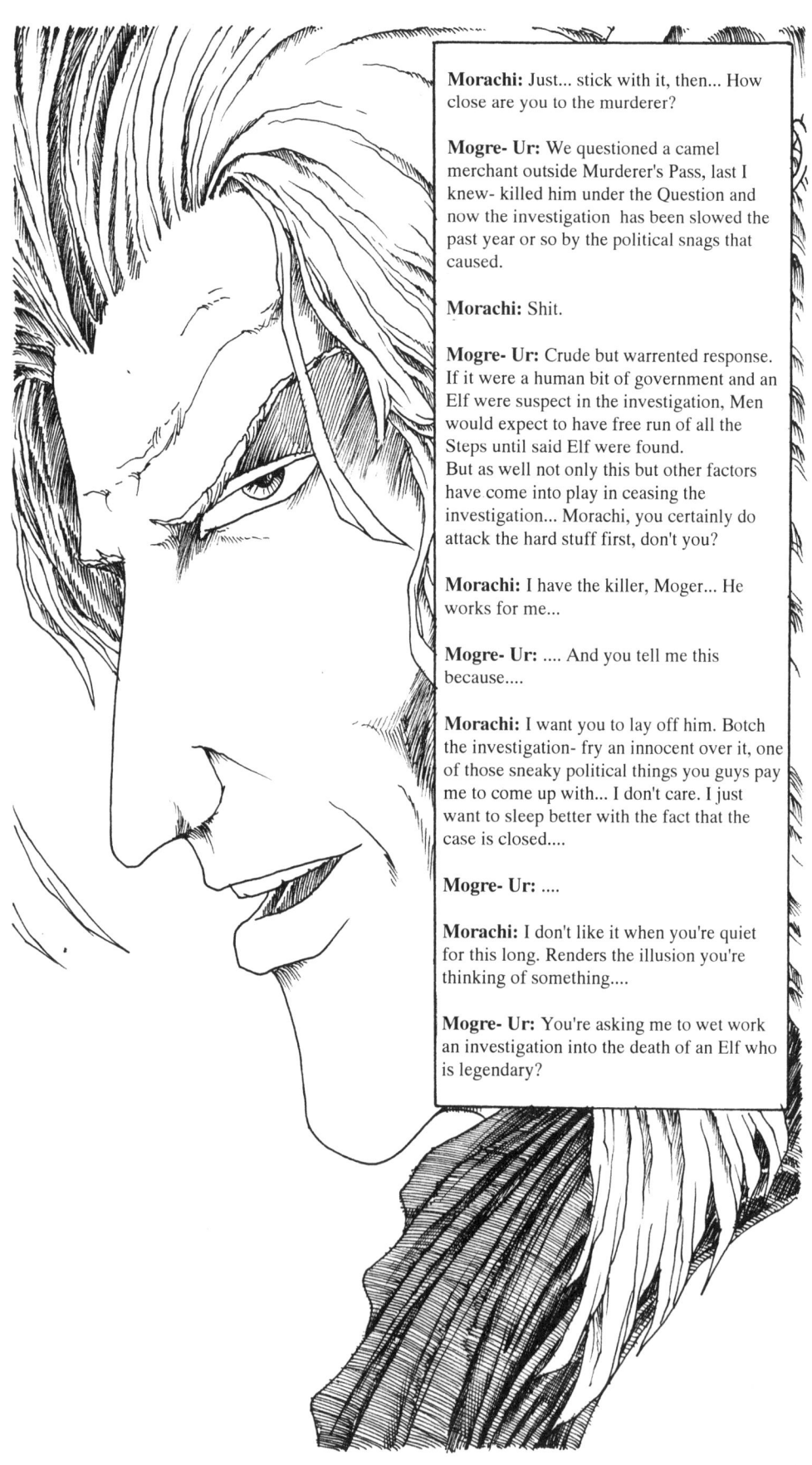

Morachi: Just... stick with it, then... How close are you to the murderer?

Mogre- Ur: We questioned a camel merchant outside Murderer's Pass, last I knew- killed him under the Question and now the investigation has been slowed the past year or so by the political snags that caused.

Morachi: Shit.

Mogre- Ur: Crude but warrented response. If it were a human bit of government and an Elf were suspect in the investigation, Men would expect to have free run of all the Steps until said Elf were found.
But as well not only this but other factors have come into play in ceasing the investigation... Morachi, you certainly do attack the hard stuff first, don't you?

Morachi: I have the killer, Moger... He works for me...

Mogre- Ur: .... And you tell me this because....

Morachi: I want you to lay off him. Botch the investigation- fry an innocent over it, one of those sneaky political things you guys pay me to come up with... I don't care. I just want to sleep better with the fact that the case is closed....

Mogre- Ur: ....

Morachi: I don't like it when you're quiet for this long. Renders the illusion you're thinking of something....

Mogre- Ur: You're asking me to wet work an investigation into the death of an Elf who is legendary?

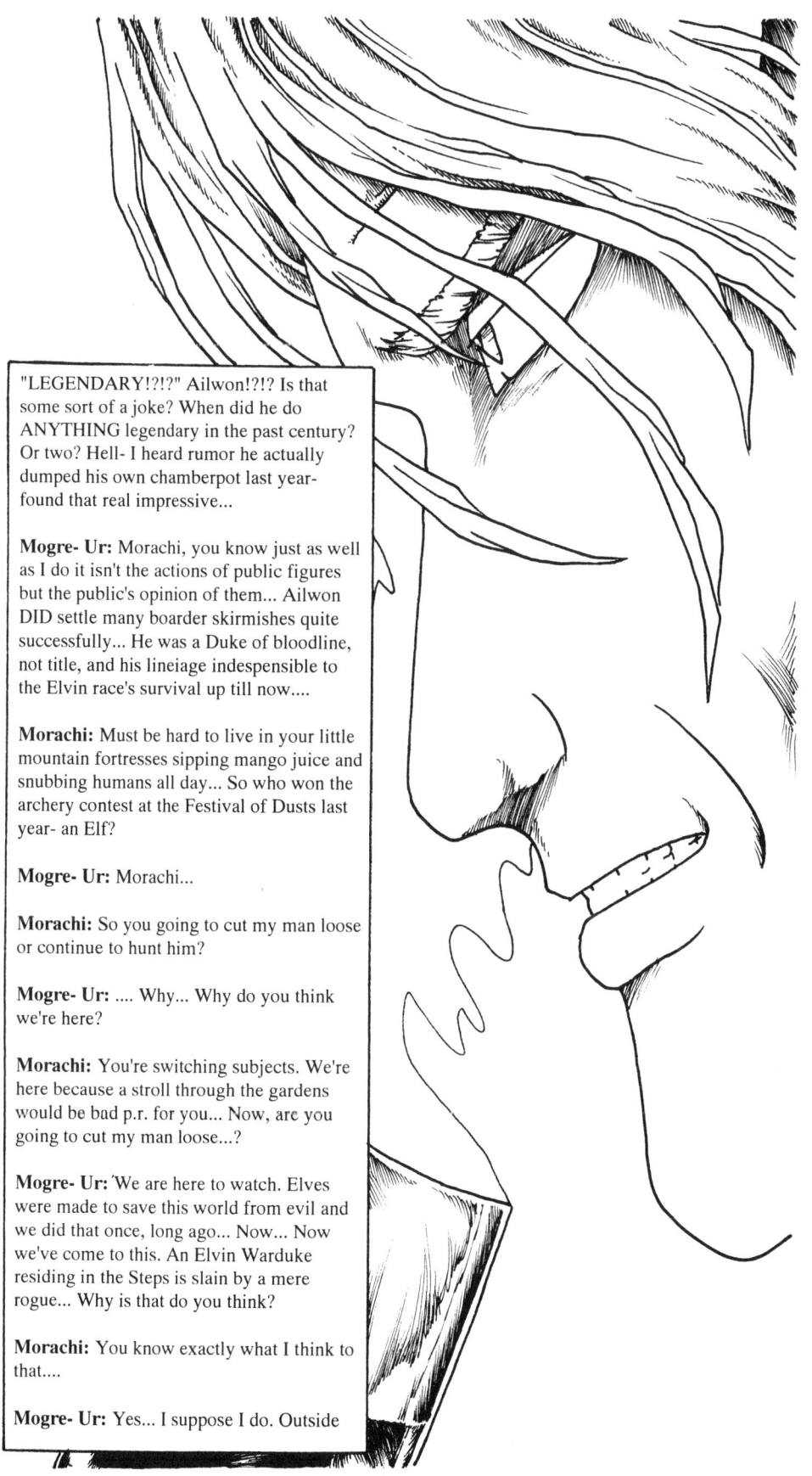

"LEGENDARY!?!?" Ailwon!?!? Is that some sort of a joke? When did he do ANYTHING legendary in the past century? Or two? Hell- I heard rumor he actually dumped his own chamberpot last year- found that real impressive...

Mogre- Ur: Morachi, you know just as well as I do it isn't the actions of public figures but the public's opinion of them... Ailwon DID settle many boarder skirmishes quite successfully... He was a Duke of bloodline, not title, and his lineage indespensible to the Elvin race's survival up till now....

Morachi: Must be hard to live in your little mountain fortresses sipping mango juice and snubbing humans all day... So who won the archery contest at the Festival of Dusts last year- an Elf?

Mogre- Ur: Morachi...

Morachi: So you going to cut my man loose or continue to hunt him?

Mogre- Ur: .... Why... Why do you think we're here?

Morachi: You're switching subjects. We're here because a stroll through the gardens would be bad p.r. for you... Now, are you going to cut my man loose...?

Mogre- Ur: 'We are here to watch. Elves were made to save this world from evil and we did that once, long ago... Now... Now we've come to this. An Elvin Warduke residing in the Steps is slain by a mere rogue... Why is that do you think?

Morachi: You know exactly what I think to that....

Mogre- Ur: Yes... I suppose I do. Outside

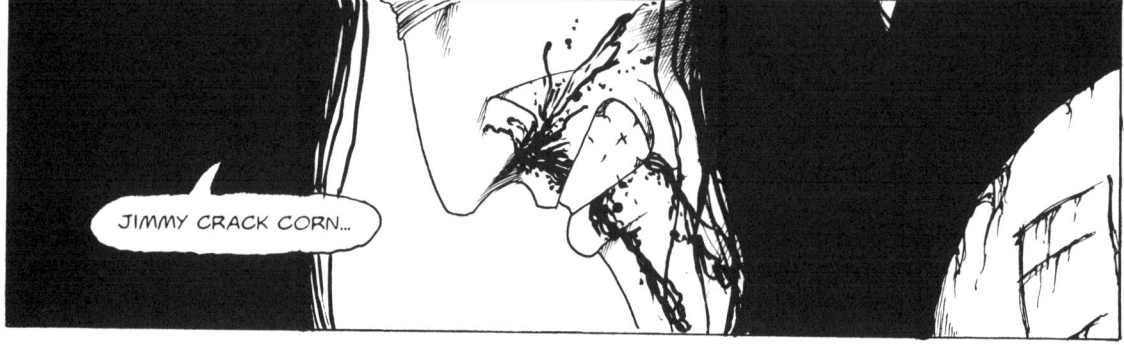

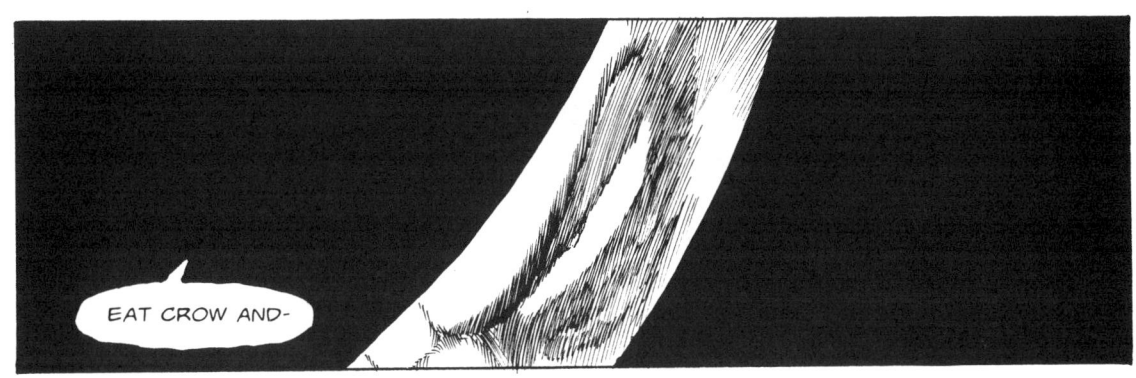

AND IN THE HANDS OF PLANNED INTERROGATION, EXPERT OR NO, THE ESCAPE TIME IS BETTER THAN HALVED. THE PAIN, INEVITABLY, CATCHES UP...

these walls spins a world most of us have grown out of touch with. We hide in these walls dilluding ourselves we're so much better than them, the rest. But when it comes down to the steel, one of us falls... Do these walls protect them from us or us from them...? Anymore... I couldn't honestly say...

Morachi: I think I could give it a shot...

Mogre- Ur: (laughs bitterly) I'm sure you could....
I will cut your man loose. He is an Elf?

Morachi: (amazed)... Uhh... Yes... He is...

Mogre- Ur: You doubtlessly wonder why I give in so easily?

Morachi: You're doubtlessly right...

Mogre- Ur: ..... Your status is now officially inactive, right?

Morachi: Yes....

Mogre- Ur: Not for long. War whispers close. You have ten months, maybe a year... Then we will need you and your brother as never before.

Morachi: Wha- whoa! Wait- slow down! What...? What is going on...?

Mogre- Ur: Goblins have been moving south for a year now. We've tried for a long time to figure out why. Human government saw to it our troops were blocked from directly encountering the Goblins to ask them ourselves- to the point they wouldn't even allow an Elvin delligation in to speak with them. They are going deep into the southern forests, hiding their actions from all. Now... Now is not the time to push the humans... Not yet....

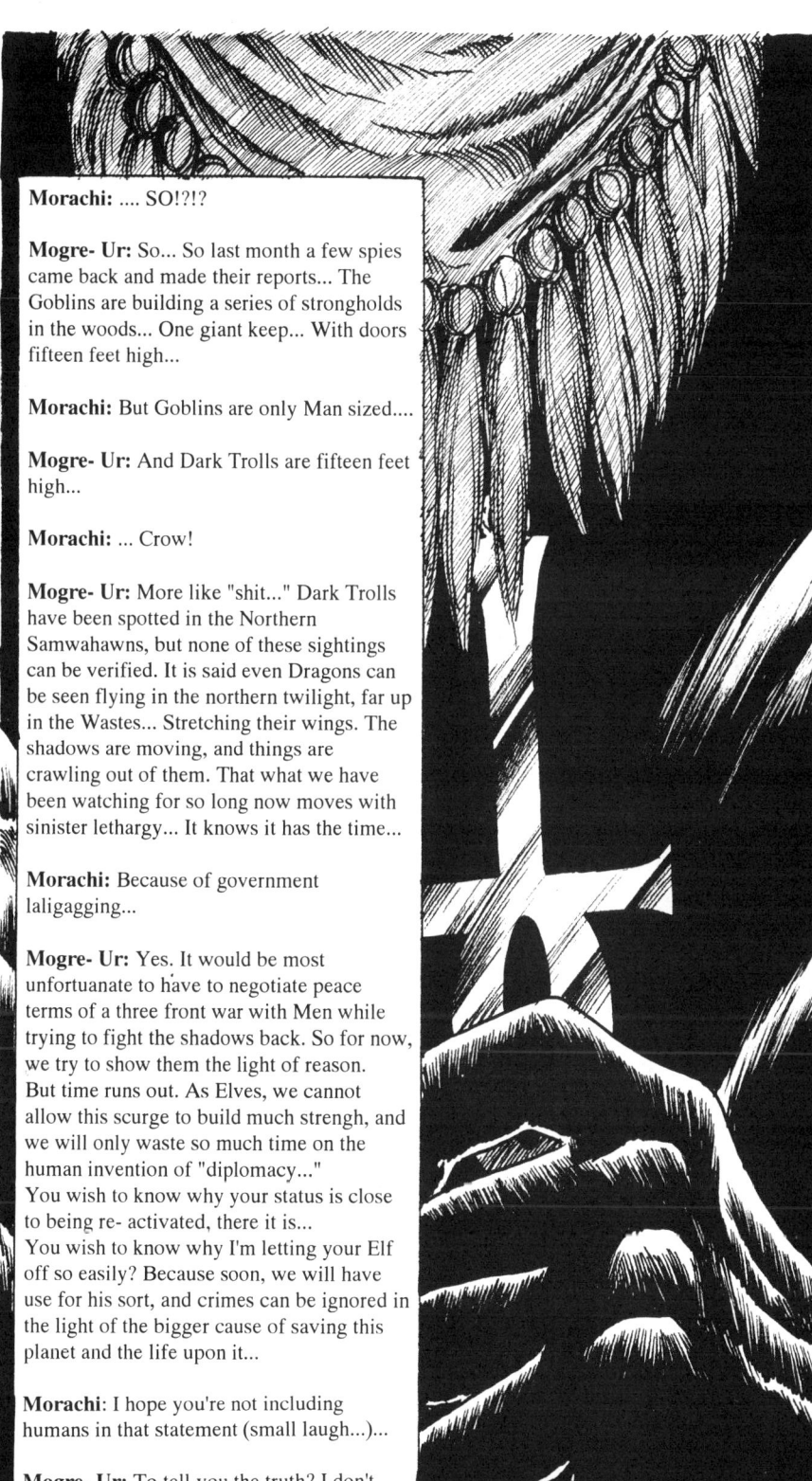

Morachi: .... SO!?!?

Mogre- Ur: So... So last month a few spies came back and made their reports... The Goblins are building a series of strongholds in the woods... One giant keep... With doors fifteen feet high...

Morachi: But Goblins are only Man sized....

Mogre- Ur: And Dark Trolls are fifteen feet high...

Morachi: ... Crow!

Mogre- Ur: More like "shit..." Dark Trolls have been spotted in the Northern Samwahawns, but none of these sightings can be verified. It is said even Dragons can be seen flying in the northern twilight, far up in the Wastes... Stretching their wings. The shadows are moving, and things are crawling out of them. That what we have been watching for so long now moves with sinister lethargy... It knows it has the time...

Morachi: Because of government laligagging...

Mogre- Ur: Yes. It would be most unfortuanate to have to negotiate peace terms of a three front war with Men while trying to fight the shadows back. So for now, we try to show them the light of reason. But time runs out. As Elves, we cannot allow this scurge to build much strengh, and we will only waste so much time on the human invention of "diplomacy..."
You wish to know why your status is close to being re- activated, there it is...
You wish to know why I'm letting your Elf off so easily? Because soon, we will have use for his sort, and crimes can be ignored in the light of the bigger cause of saving this planet and the life upon it...

Morachi: I hope you're not including humans in that statement (small laugh...)...

Mogre- Ur: To tell you the truth? I don't think I care much for the thought of humans surviving into the new age... But then, this is just talk for now...

Morachi: Uh- huh....

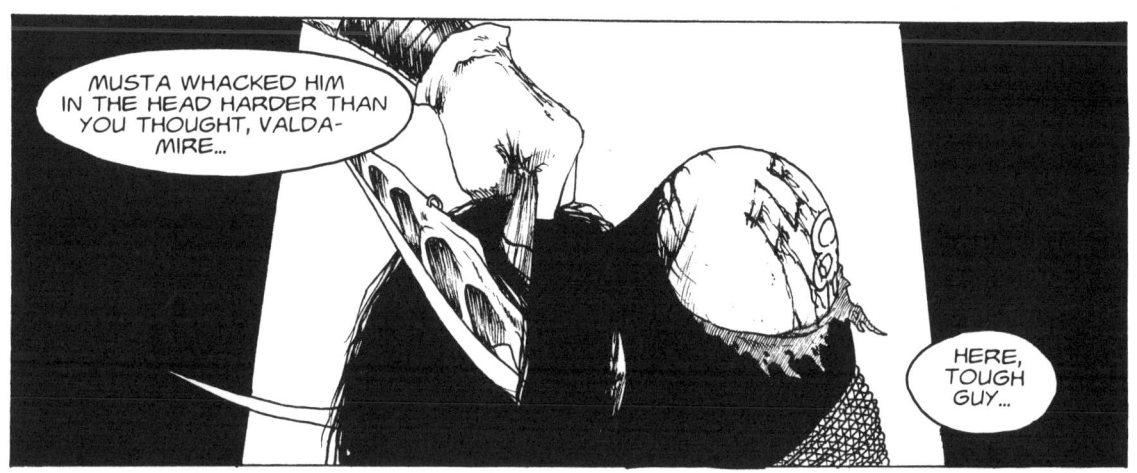

COME IN AND PLAY WITH US...!

HEY!

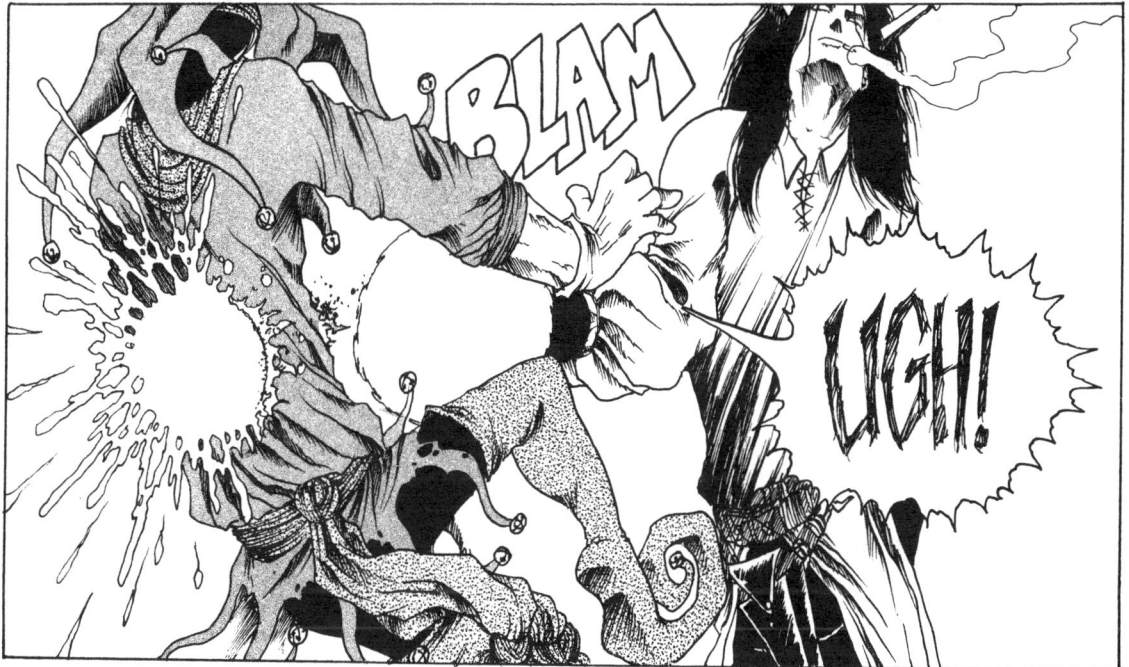
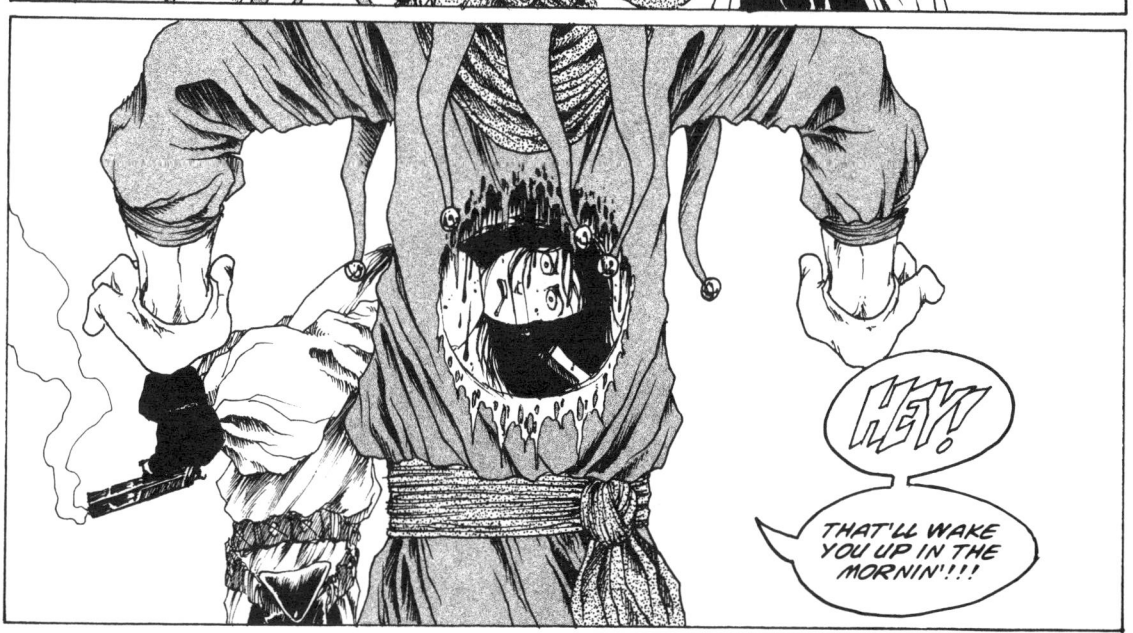

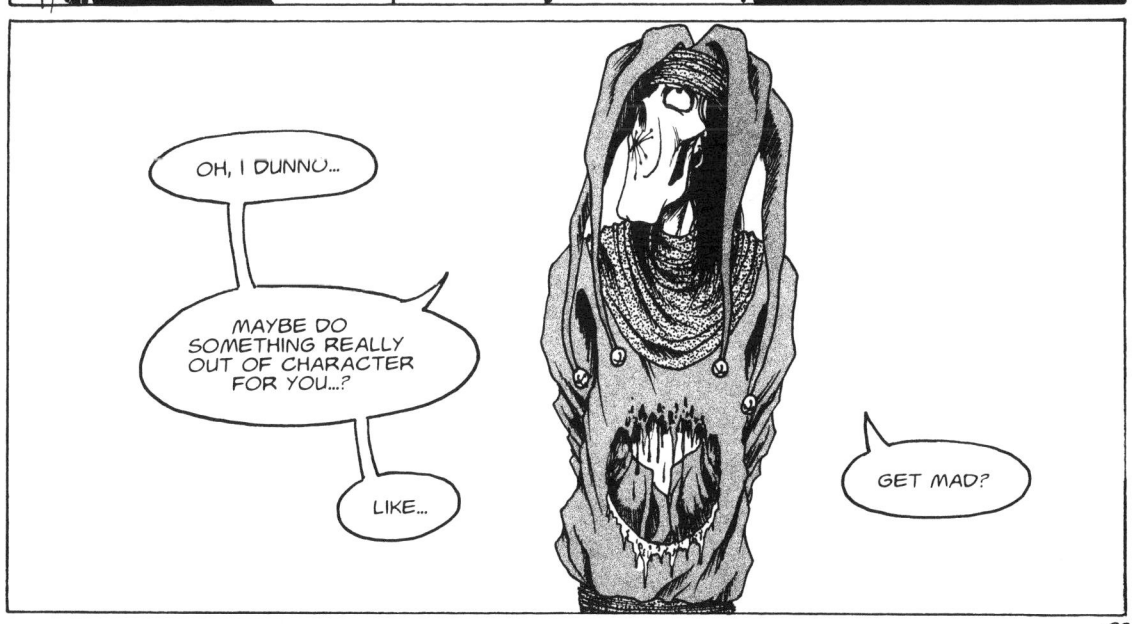

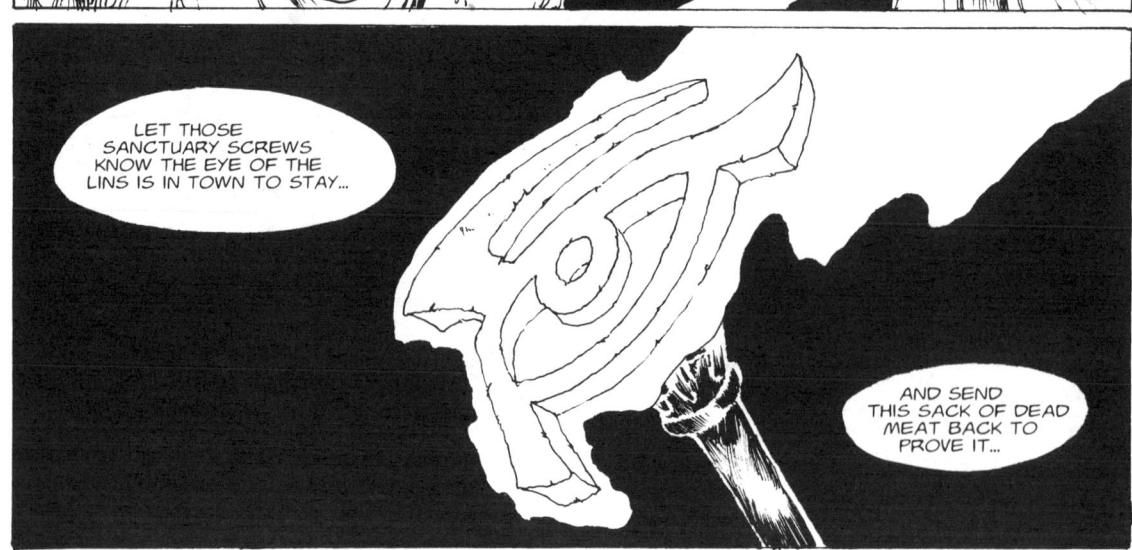

"YOU BOYS— ALL YOU BOYS...

SAY GOOD-NIGHT TO THE SANDMAN..."

THREE

DEATH

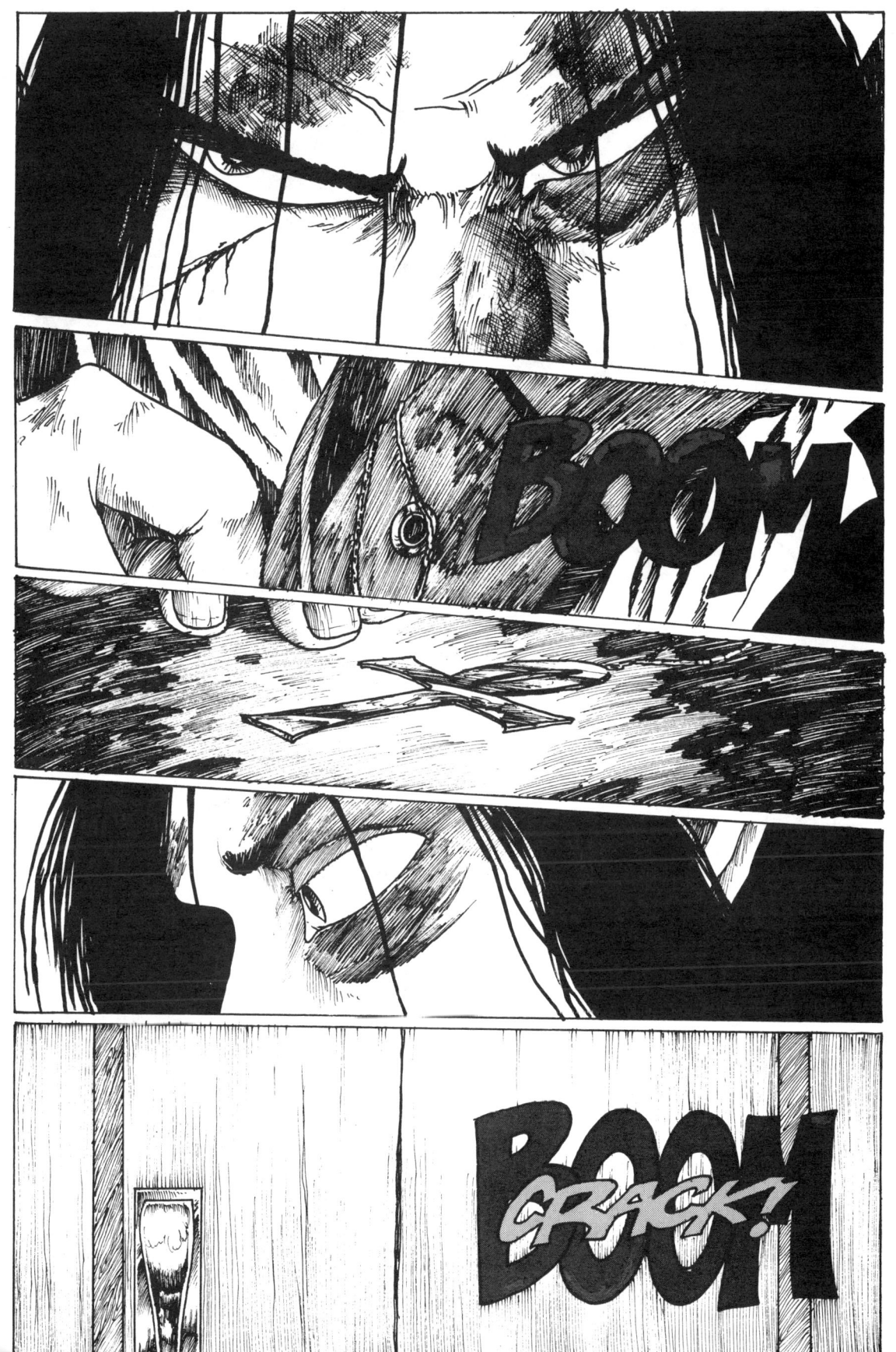

HAH!

CRACK!

HEH!

FOUR

INQUISITION

Vido: Alright, me lovelies- calm down... You in the back, sit down or I'll have you shot...

(Laughter about the room)

Perry: It's cold out, sir- why do you call us out on a cold, Sunday morning..?

Vido: because I'm the meanest pig in Mandratha. Now Daniels? Shoot him...

(More laughter...)

Vido: Alright, seriously... The reason I've called this meeting is we have less than one year to catch a Sanctuary thief or assassin- preferably assassin, or it's back to rousing hookers and drunks for you sorry- asses. Up till recently, police investigation has been a lot of policing and very little investigating. I'm sorry to say but the eyes of the world are upon us. What we are attempting is unique but long overdue- trying to catch criminals after the fact of the crime, not during, and catching them with evidence of that crime despite whether or not they have confessed. First of all, since we're all here, let us formally welcome the Golden Boy, our newest member of the Blood Guard, Jace...

(Muttered welcomes from the other six in the room. Jace silently nods and lifts, drops a hand. Yeah, yeah...)

Vido: Jace, as you may have noticed, or you're fired, is an Elf. Let us hope that this new blood will offer a different perspective and wisdom to our little quest, here. Now, Daniels is going to fill you in on a few things- then I've got a surprise for you...

(Vido goes to side of boardroom and sits, while Daniels rises and clears throat.)

Daniels: You all may remember back a while

ago, Jace- you've read this file? The Dwarven assassin incident from a couple months ago. While we determined this was not a Sanctuary hit it was a little too weird to be not connected in some way to these people. There has been no new leads on where the Dwarf came from, but his body WAS discovered on the west side full of strange bullets...

(Daniels holds up a spent .45 slug)

Daniels: Anyone ever seen anything like this? We pried a few out of the dead girl and the other bodies in the crime scene as well as out of the walls of the apartment. These bullets are sure to be generated from the gun of the Elf the Dwarf was apparently pursuing. There has been no sign of this Elf since... All names we've attempted to trace have been false....

(Vido gives Daniels a look and Daniels clears throat again...)

Daniels: Well, Vido will get you back to that. Within the past month, the assassination rate in this city has doubled. It is rumored on the streets another guild has moved into town and is setting up shop. We expect many things to result of this... Yeah, Duke?

Duke: One of my contacts claims this other guild caught a Sanctuary member.

Kemper: Bullshit.

Wally: No way.

Smithers: If WE can't do it how can they?

Jace: Maybe they know how Sanctuary works better than we do.

Duke: Exactly. As much as we'd like to think they love us, we're still cops, and our street people may not be giving us as good a

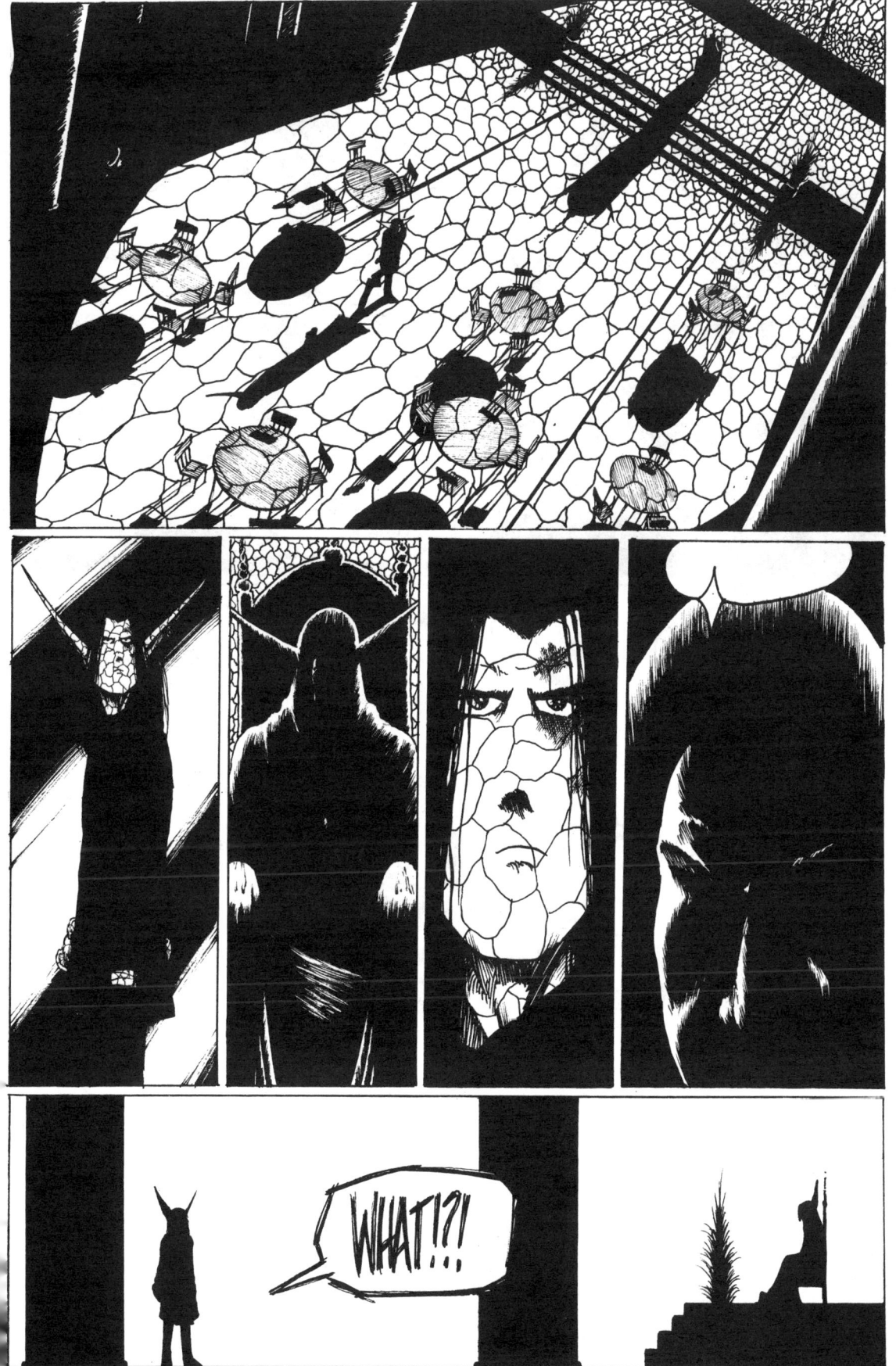

information as we'd like to think.

Kemper: I still think that's a load of crap.

Vido (rising): Gentlemen, what it is at this point is rumor and conjecture. We hear rumors but do not listen. When rumor proves to be fact, we react, but we will not waste our time chasing ghosts, or nitpicking eachother over them. While it's perfectly reasonable abducting a Sanctuary member would be easier for them than us on the basis of street contacts, I highly doubt it. The luck involved would still have to be phenomenal.

Kemper: Yeah, it's all opinion anyway, and opinions are like assholes.

Vido: And it's your opinions that make you an asshole, Kemp. When you have a good one, share. But for now- shut up, quit playing the coffeehouse pessimist, and listen...

(Kemper immediately falls into a dark part of Kemperland.)

Daniels (clears throat again): Alright- lemme finish up before this cold starts killing my voice. We've been fairly good at dividing the murders lately into our four categories: pedestrian, Sanctuary, suicide, and unknown. Unknown has moved along with little change and we'll continue to watch these for any signs of Sanctuary. Sanctuary crime scenes themselves have remained much the same. Body, some signs of break in, no evidence, and no signs of leaving- this leads us to believe some sort of sorcery may be involved in their get away procedure. Recently, an event has confirmed this....

(Small gasps and wake up noises abound throughout the room. Daniels sits and Vido rises.)

Vido: Five and a half years we have looked and found no trace nor witness to anything Sanctuary related. Well, gentlemen, now we have something...

(Dramatic pause... Room is silent.)

Vido: Two weeks ago in a back alley four blocks down from, yes, THIS building, Anton Hazelwood crumb, a homeless vagrant, was sleeping behind a garbage bin in the snow when a group of thieves entered the alley plaza. Mention was made to Sanctuary and a thief was named in connection- Denrin to Anton's best recollection. After a half hour another individual walked onto the scene. Denrin marked this person, an Elf, as a Sanctuary assassin...

(Ohhs and ahhs whisper...)

Vido: Yes, kiddies. Said assassin proceeded then to systematically wipe out everyone in the alley save Denrin- our witness claims the assassin moved with a speed he'd never before believed possible. When it was over, the assassin nailed the thief to the wall with his swords, held muttered conversation with him, and let him go. The assassin left on his own two feet the way he'd come in...
The thief, on the other hand, pulled a necklace from his throat and disappeared.

(Silence.)

Vido: The Elf, as Anton describes him, is a perfect match for the one involved in the #138 massacre....

(Jace slumps unnoticeably down in chair...)

SECOND SHOT

SO...

AW, MAN...

HUH...

MAN...

HEART KICKING IN A BIT?

YOU NEED TO KNOW ONE THING— WHAT *I* NEED TO KNOW...

AND THAT'S THE LOCATION OF YOUR GUILD...

I'M NOT GOING TO SIT HERE LIKE SOME *PARROT* REPEATING MYSELF...

SAME QUESTION OVER AND OVER AGAIN...

BUT WHEN YOU'RE *READY*, YOU TELL ME, AND WE'LL QUIT...

HEH...

NO WAY...

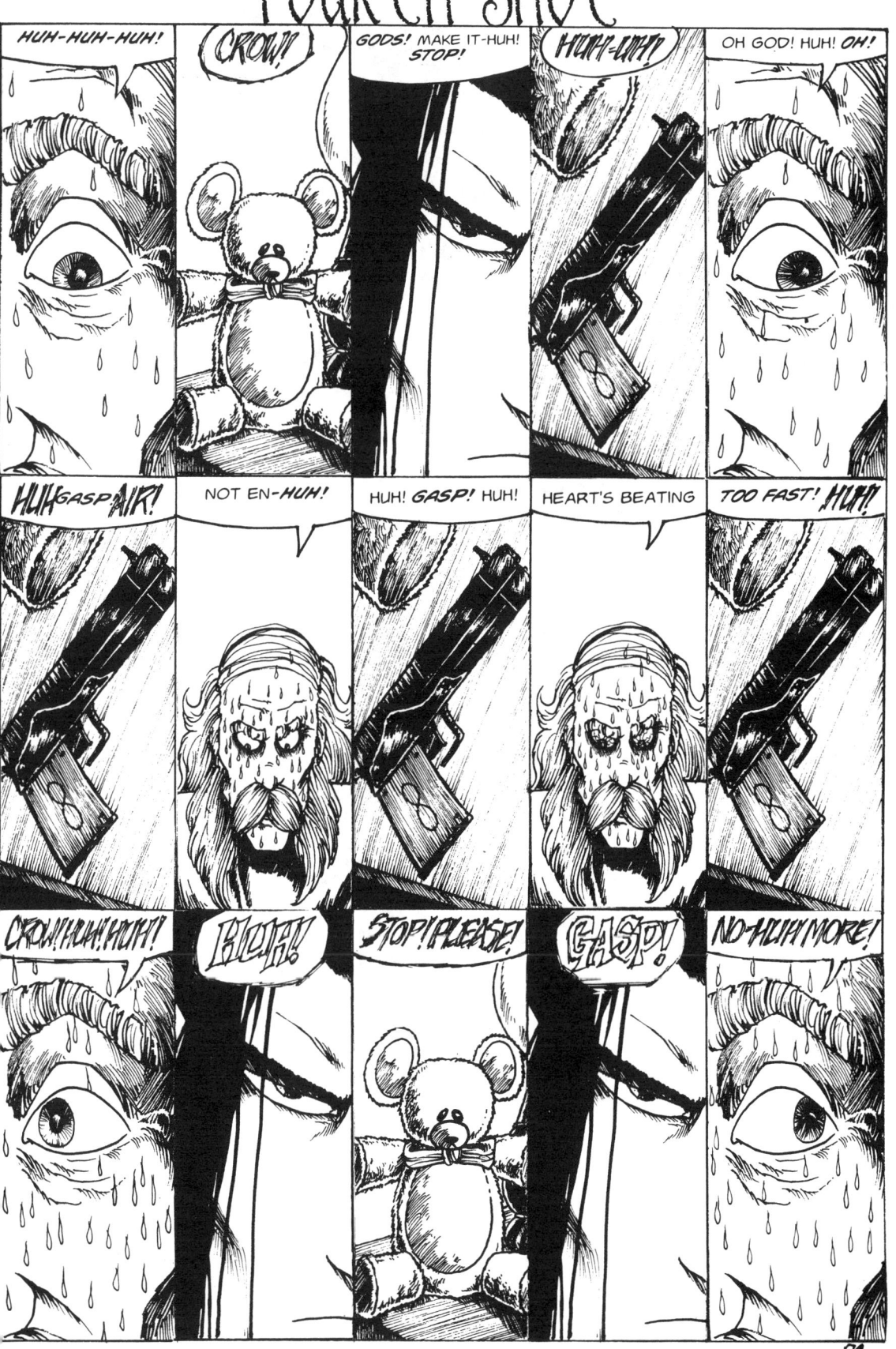

FIVE

BLOODHOUNDS

Lusiphur sat on the edge of his bed smoking, watching tendrils of grey smoke dance up slowly to the ceiling. Occasionally he'd obliterate the graceful twirls with a blast of exhale, a forceful plume of smoke that, after two or so feet, would slow and begin its lazy ascent again. He stared at the smoke, drawing from his cigarette again and again, letting his mind relax.

Hell of a gig tonight.

The sounds of booted feet marching determined past his door had edged off. Now only once in awhile would he hear a scampering down the hall of someone thinking they were late, hasty, not wanting to miss anything. Once in awhile a fist would slam into his door and a cry heard, "WOOOO! LUSE! GONNA KICK SOME ASS!" To which Lusiphur would let fly with a string of ballsey profanity usually ushering a guffaw out of whoever was banging on his door. Then they'd run off to join the others in the main hall.

He was almost done anyway. He sat wrapped in leather and metal. He surveyed.

Working up his right leg around his calf were strapped seven throwing knives inside his boot. On his upper thigh was strapped his gun connected to his gun belt, around which he kept packs of poisons, various odds and ends like string, needles, skeleton keys, wire, Imp's claw, field bandages, oils- anything that he may need in the weirdest situations but might be caught short of.

Crossing this belt was his sword belt, off which to the side hung Sinlach, his useless magic sword, and other knives (his big knife he took to calling the "General" lately was at the small of his back). Down his left leg was a dagger strapped to his upper thigh, his calf, and inside his boot was another knife made more for hardware use than killing (though it'd do fine there...). His ankles themselves were reinforced, as were his wrists and rib cage, with black strands of leather.

Over his trunk lay the bands of leather to his chest, a black padded undershirt over which he threw his chainmail shirt over which he wore a black, long-sleeved affair. Gloves were pulled up to his elbows and under each was strapped a long knife. For killing.

His hood rested over his shoulders and was hard, black studded leather. Over this he slung his bandolier of packs, throwing knives, and two smoke grenades. Around his neck was his ankh, over his head pinning his ears to the side was a black bandanna. His cigarette was in his right hand, the rest of his hood in the left.

Sometimes here he sat and though deeply about his life and could scarcely believe where he was. What he was doing. Just a short time ago he'd been retired. Long retired as an assassin but had hung up the sword for good. Now he didn't remember why. Too many lost chances? The trouble it brought?

He slumped his head in his hands. *Crow, not this self-pitying shit again...* He thought.

In fact, Lusiphur figured out awhile ago why he'd decided to retire. And why he came out.

Living by the sword gets into your blood. You watch people- what society calls "regular" people- sift through their lives, shuffle down the street. What are you supposed to do with your life? This. This is it. You grow up institutionalized. You

do this, you don't dare do that. You kill your creativity and slay the adventurer within yourself with the limitations society puts on you. You're programmed from day one that THIS is how you should be. You're supposed to let yourself be molded into a cog to run in the world's living machine that is celebrated as "society."

He'd watch people when he was young, living on the streets, unbeknownst to him free from this barrage. Free from being molded. He'd watch people go to work. He'd watch them come home. Their wives. Their children. Distractions to the mundanities of their lives were pathetic at best. They were suckered full and to the hilt so deep in it they didn't even know it anymore. Maybe if they could see that youth within themselves again, the person that was only half dogged but still had a fighting chance- maybe if they could see that person they could come out of it. Free themselves.

No. They couldn't really. They'd see all the things they wanted to do, all the things they could have done, all the things they missed out on solely because they were letting themselves be molded. Feeling they *had* to let themselves be molded. Letting their dreams die through complacency and idleness and weakness one by one until their only dream was to achieve some position in society.

They'd see all that and kill themselves.

People are like lemmings. They really are. Watch them. All of them, even some of your friends. Maybe even you. Scampering along in life chasing each golden ring we all must have to reach the next step up towards being socially acceptable. Functional. Jumping through all its hoops and leaving their dreams and ambitions behind for the dreams and ambitions society tells them to have. You can't paint for a living! You can do it as a hobby- something to distract yourself from the mundanity of your life, but don't dare try to make a living at it. That's not society- that's the self...

Society is not constructed for the artists' survival. You have to have a job to pay your bills, rent, to eat. Work occupies eight to ten of most peoples' sixteen hours of wakefulness. When you get home from work the last thing you can think about is painting after that. You want to spend the rest of your waking hours forgetting the fact that you have a shit job you hate doing something you have no interest in for a boss who's most concern for you is if you're going to show up the next day. That and you're dead beat anyway so you distract yourself from your current life not with your dreams, or pursuing them- because that inspiration is dying day by day anyway- but you distract yourself with the other components society says you should have. Wife. Children. Friends.

So instead of picking up a brush you can worry about getting laid or drunk or cowing to someone else's demons but never chasing your own.

And Lusiphur considered himself an artist.

Because artists are rogues, or rogues are artists- he didn't philosophize this into the ground. It was simply that there were people who could exist and live and even thrive within the smothering confines of society and those who couldn't. The fallout of this whole thing were those that blindly went against society even if it was going against something within them, simply for the sake of saying, "Since this is a part of society, I am NOT going to follow it or be *THAT* way!"

Talk about VICTIMS of society. These were society's most pathetic and blind

whipping children.

But Lusiphur had no doubts about it. He wasn't fooling himself. He could simply not live in society for long. He could try- he often did- but he was too far diverse from it. Not because of what it did to him or expected but because he was naturally that way.

It was like the difference between those that refuse to believe in God because society put that on them and they're blindly rebelling but hoping inside that if there is one that "He" doesn't hold that thinking against them, and someone who doesn't believe in God and doesn't worry about forgiveness for it.

Because to them there really was no God to forgive.

He knew this for so long. He also saw MANY people who were such products of society while saying they hated it or weren't part of it that it was sometimes a sad joke. They were the most dependant on society because without it they would have no identity.

But Lusiphur knew he was always outside of it. He was not a senseless, blind heathen nor a rebel. He was a misfit. He didn't need people. He didn't act like a misanthrope and collect friends. He simply did not work in society.

Lusiphur did not act like normal people. He didn't share their concerns or fears and all of his they were too blind to see because they were, as far as he was concerned, strangers to this world. The same world they all lived in but he saw differently and very few could relate. What mattered to him was a joke to them. His fears they called "paranoia." His loves were silly and stupid. His past pains were a tired, old story that tore at him almost daily. He felt alone most of the time. He didn't mind it.

And retirement? Retirement from the sword was a grasp at the phantom illusion of society his early years had tried to program him to assimilate into. It was fooling himself into thinking he was better, or worse, than he thought he was. That he could be "normal."

Sometimes.. A lot of times, he felt alien- even with Cassy.

Cassy. Crow, what a frickin' light in his life right now. Blood on his hands, paid with money shadowed in murder, living under a roof of people who brought pain and death to others for profit, and him and she amongst them. One of them.

At first he'd been impressed with her in general, which for him with women was rare. Women who are impressive tend to realize it fairly early in life and hone that to a fine point so they're either incredibly insecure about it, be it looks, common sense, or whatever- or they're plain evil about it. At least men are consistently moronic.

Cassy impressed him beyond words and not for the reasons one may associate with her looks. Good looking women were a dime a dozen and he'd seen enough of them naked to know there were things that were more intrinsic to long-lasting affairs than an aesthetically pleasing package. A good looking woman with nothing else- no brains, no honor, no integrity, no perception or insight- was only good for one thing. A thing that he only looked at as a damn fine fringe benefit with Cass.

She had the strength to accept him, broken bits and all, without judging him or making him feel bad about the way he was. Lusiphur knew he was screwed up. He

knew he was pathological, dark and morose, sardonic about himself and the world, lacking faith in anything let alone another being. He also knew he was quite beyond "fixing."

And this was the funny part that when he really thought about it, which was probably not often enough, made him want to bleed for her. She cared enough to know he was beyond fixing but trusted that while he couldn't ever become an emotionally balanced person for all, he would learn to trust her. She didn't care if he trusted anyone else, as long as he trusted her.

There were things buried deep in Luse's psyche. Things that couldn't be looked at directly. Things he couldn't put into words but still tortured him- being this close to someone- that were often taken out on that someone. These things were past hurts and current effects he could never explain to another nor to himself but only judge that she was worth it.

He could get over these things for her and only for her, and never for anyone else. And he knew she'd give her time to.

And tonight where was she?

Meeting with Morachi, Lufgow, and Talon while the rest of Sanctuary's members waited in the main hall. When the two leaders and their lieutenants come out of meeting, they will all be teleported to Serendeh as one, Lusiphur among them, two blocks down from the Eye of the Lins' main hideout. Sanctuary would then proceed to eradicate the opposing guild from the face of the planet.

Morachi had never before tolerated opposing guilds in his city until Vido started the Bloodguard. It was only typical for the occasional rotter to figure he could push the Thief King out or force Morachi to share his town, with hopes of someday overthrowing him completely.

But since the Bloodguard, things got trickier, and so did Morachi. For one year straight he had Vido convinced he'd caught the Sanctuary. Problem was, Sanctuary assassins and thieves were just too professional.

Holding up the average assassin to an assassin of Lusiphur's caliber was like holding a moth to a butterfly. Most guilds were built with one butterfly surrounded by moths, as everyone figured the Eye of the Lins was. Assassins who you give a knife and a crown and say, "Go kill him!" And he'll do it with little suave or talent. These are the idiots you hear about coming after government officials during campaign speeches and such, "Assassin dies in attempt to kill Mayor Shitcreek" or whatever.

Professionals knew better than take hits on politicians. Royalty you could knock off any day and it's one less King or Queen- politicians actually mattered.

It was also a move of the amateur to capture a member of a professional guild and not kill him immediately. And to have expected Luse to divulge anything about Sanctuary was a move on the part of stupidity as well.

Lusiphur stood up and felt the weight of metal and leather pulling at his body, making him feel like a machine. He cracked his neck and flexed his shoulders, feeling the dull throb of the brand those bastards had put on him. That stupid Eye. He clenched his left fist and right, cigarette in mouth, and felt like his fists could blast through steel. He felt like a knot of destruction, wound up and ready to be released.

He didn't fear violence or regret it- he loved it and had to admit that, time allowing with situation, nothing made him feel better than breaking some moron's neck.

The elf crushed out his cigarette in an ashtray and exhaled the last breath of smoke.

Retirement had been a last grab for the remnants of what society had put into him. Cassy was what gave him hope he could, for someone caring enough, be caring back. Sanctuary gave him his strength and brotherhood.

He felt like he could take on the Tenth Legion right now...

And this other guild was going to hurt tonight.

SIX

REVELATION

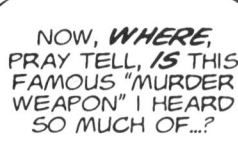

BACK OFF!

ALRIGHT.

JACE, STAY IN HERE WITH WAL...

JUST ONE OF YOU BASTARDS EVEN TOUCHES ME YOU'LL BE ROUSTING MIDGETS OUT OF FIXED DWARF TOSSING MEETS!

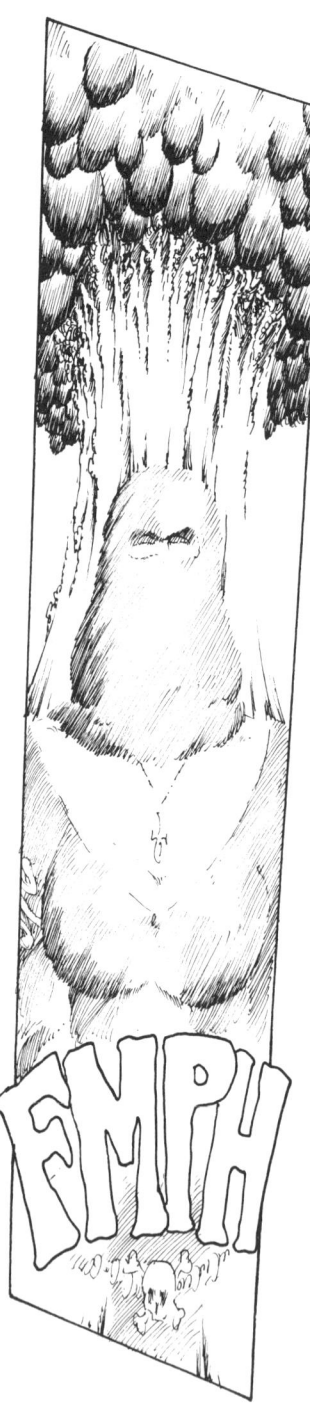

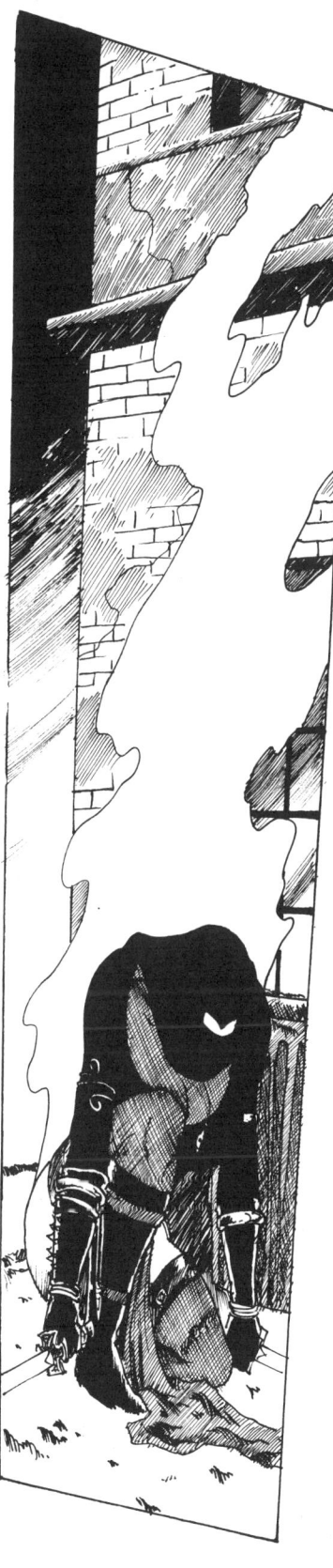

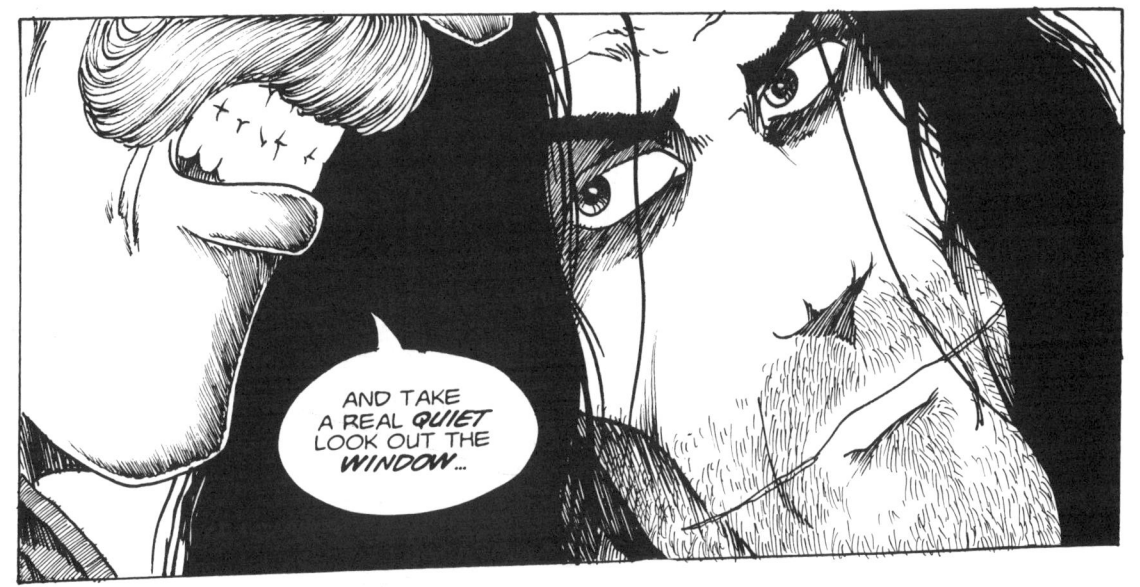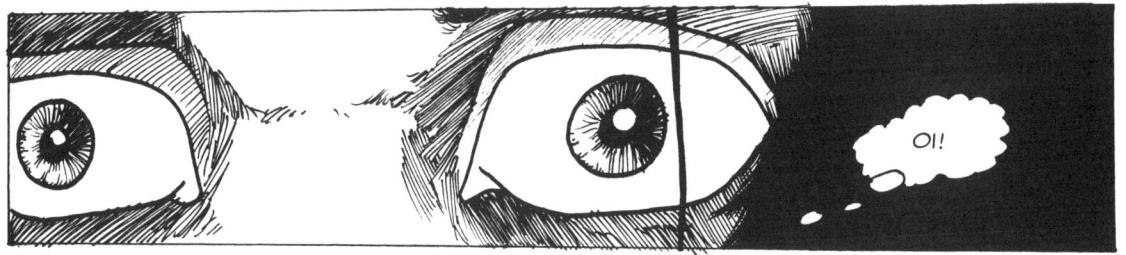

SEVEN

RETRIBUTION

The night was partly cloudy, the full moon giving off a bluish glow to the city's snow covered streets. A cold, bitter wind whispered through the buildings, blowing forth occasional snow-devils, freezing momentarily the breath of anyone so foolish to be out.

The War of the Mandratha Guilds was a complicated night indeed. The Eye of the Lins sat in a fortified warehouse of which from all outside appearances seemed abandoned. Surrounding this was Sanctuary en masse... Surrounding Sanctuary was 39 armed Mandratha Guard headed by four of the Bloodgaurd...

Vido's instructions were precise and to the point... Wait for the signal to attack- anyone jumping the gun prematurely would be brought up on charges of treason against state in the high court of Mandratha... Once the attack commenced, there would be a scatter- concentrate on Sanctuary members only- they'd be the ones in black- capture them alive if possible, but dead was fine... Any guard managing this would receive every reward Lieutenant Vido would be able to bestow or seen bestowed upon them. Vido made no illusions about his desperation and desire in this hour. What had been dropped into his lap was the proverbial magic beans, and it was up to him to see they grew.

His intentions were to let Sanctuary go about their business and interrupt halfway through. Let a little fight get taken out of them and hopefully their numbers thinned- but he doubted that. This new guild were full of half-ass dandies mostly. Second rate thieves and maybe two or three assassins terribly under trained. Vido saw Sanctuary moving silently through the snow- black apparitions on a sea of ice, crawling building tops and ledges fading in and out of shadows, and he knew he'd be facing them all- that none of these other guildsmen would survive their attack.

THESE were professionals and what Vido had measured himself against over the years. He would always be an amateur until he brought them down. These were the things that went bump in the night, the shifting shadow in the dark of the closet- the bogeymen. The thieves he could care less about. Some rich asshole's jewelry collection gets pilfered, well- bastard shouldda hocked a few rocks for a decent safe. The assassins were the takers of life. Lives that Vido had sworn an oath to protect almost twenty years ago. You could die on his beat, but god forbid you killed.

And as the last hour of the Eye of the Lins grew shorter, so did Vido's temper, then sanity. He took on a voice not unlike a cobra's about to strike. His hands shook and eyes darted. All had to go off as planned. This was an impossible opportunity and he would NOT let anything or anyone mess it up. He was smelling Sanctuary and salivated like a werewolf at the scent of virgin blood.

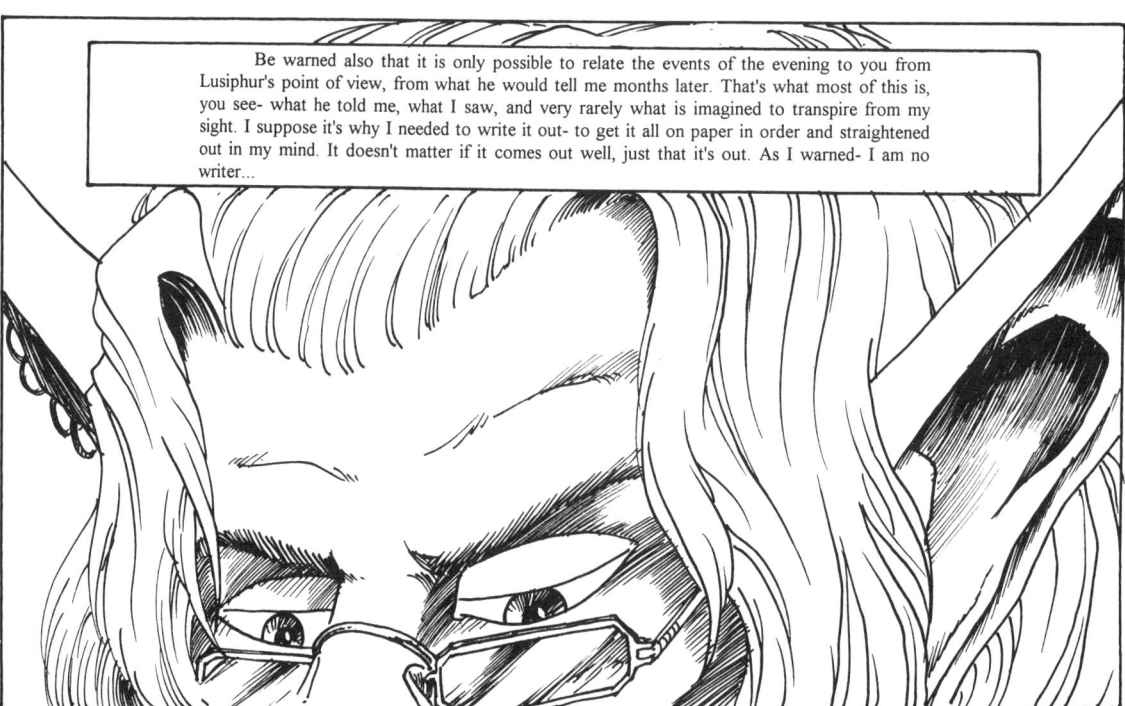

Be warned also that it is only possible to relate the events of the evening to you from Lusiphur's point of view, from what he would tell me months later. That's what most of this is, you see- what he told me, what I saw, and very rarely what is imagined to transpire from my sight. I suppose it's why I needed to write it out- to get it all on paper in order and straightened out in my mind. It doesn't matter if it comes out well, just that it's out. As I warned- I am no writer...

LUSE'S JOB WAS TO PICK OFF ANYONE RUNNING AWAY.

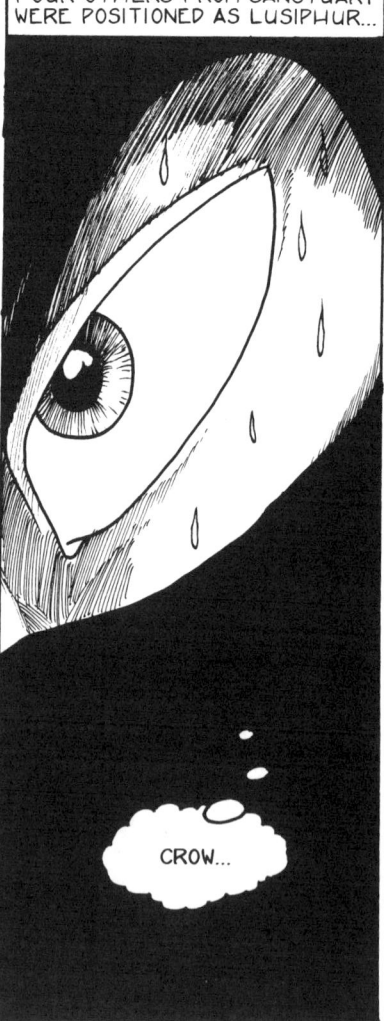

FOUR OTHERS FROM SANCTUARY WERE POSITIONED AS LUSIPHUR...

CROW...

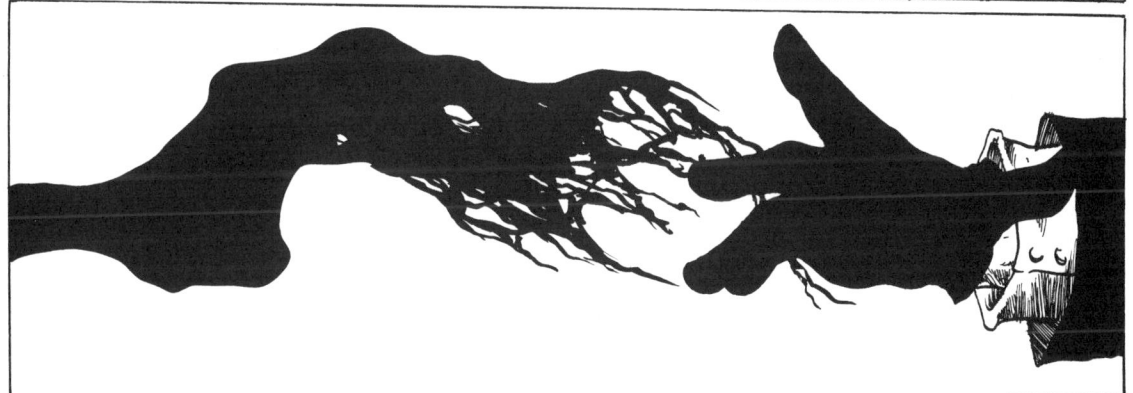

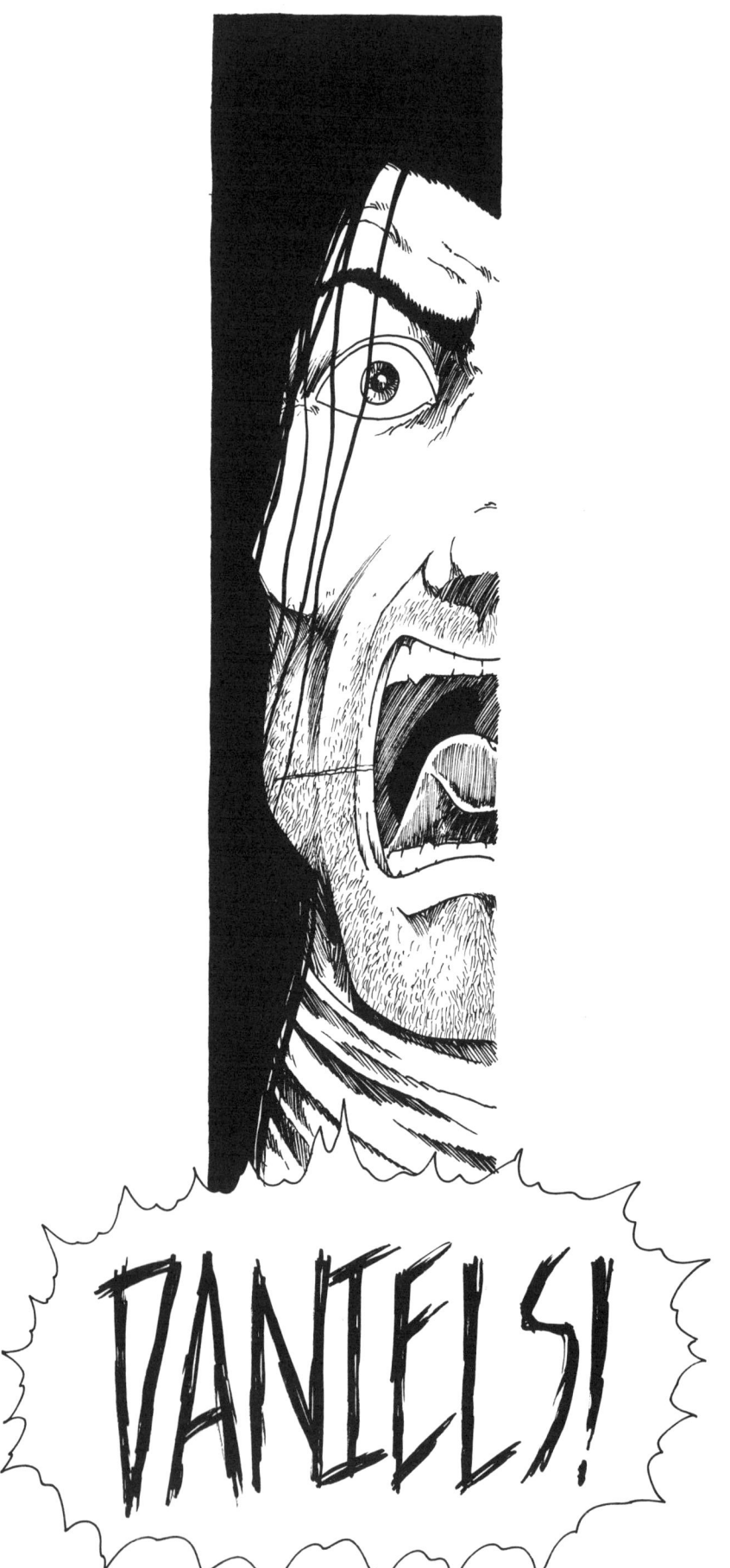

21st PRECINCT, MANDRATHA

SANCTUARY

book four

STRANGE DAYS

ONE

NO NEW TALE TO TELL

MANDRATHA CITY, NORTHERN GATE PROPER...

SO I HEAR THE MAYOR HAS EVEN GOT OFF HIS ASS...

YEP — THAT'S THE WORD

DIDN'T YOU SERVE WITH DANIELS...?

YEP.

TEN YEARS AGO...

HEY!

LOOKEE THAT...

SANCTUARY - CASSY'S BEDROOM...

TWO

SECOND COMINGS

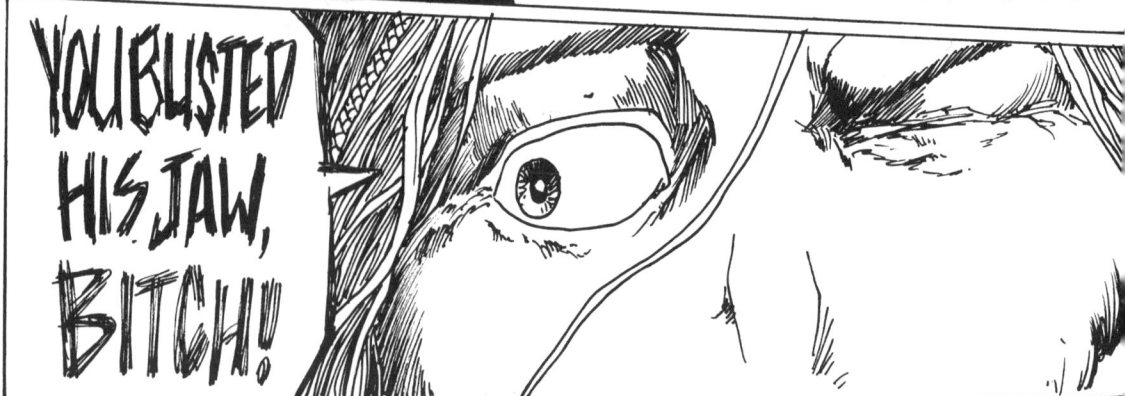

Talon stared into space brooding.

Morachi's office was thick with the smell of cigar and the sense of oppression. The raid on the Eye of the Lins had gone almost well except for two things- they all hadn't teleported at once and Lusiphur had killed one of Vido's men- in front of Vido...

Lusiphur....

The subject was a rough one. Morachi put his head in his hands. His wife was arriving anytime into this mess and now, on top of everything, the Thief King had to admit the worst.... He'd been wrong.

The reasons they didn't all teleport away at once were debatable and innumerable but they all meant the same thing- whatever it was, that many of Sanctuary should never try to get back at once. It was a full ten minutes before everyone was home. Simple. Don't go out like that again....

Now Lusiphur.... This was much touchier...

He was a square peg in a round hole. He was a misfit in the truest sense, and one that could destroy all he and Talon had worked to build...

Sure, it was genius at first. After several marginally successful but always thwarted attempts the brothers had stumbled across the thought that if a guild weren't on the Prime it could virtually NEVER be found by the cops. Put the structure on another dimension- a slip between time and space. Provide a means for the assassins and thieves to migrate back and forth. Protect it from magical prying eyes.

This is where their Mage Serendeh Sol Nalhide came in....

Into every criminals' life a little bounty must fall, and Serendeh was theirs. A powerful Wizard whose boredom of all had recently peaked. When Morachi offered him a salary and a chance to hide from the Prime, meditate indefinitely, the Mage accepted the position with great enthusiasm. It was never determined before now the limit of his powers, and an apology was definitely in order for accidentally doing so.

* APOLOGIES TO THE MIGHTY JEFFREY JONES

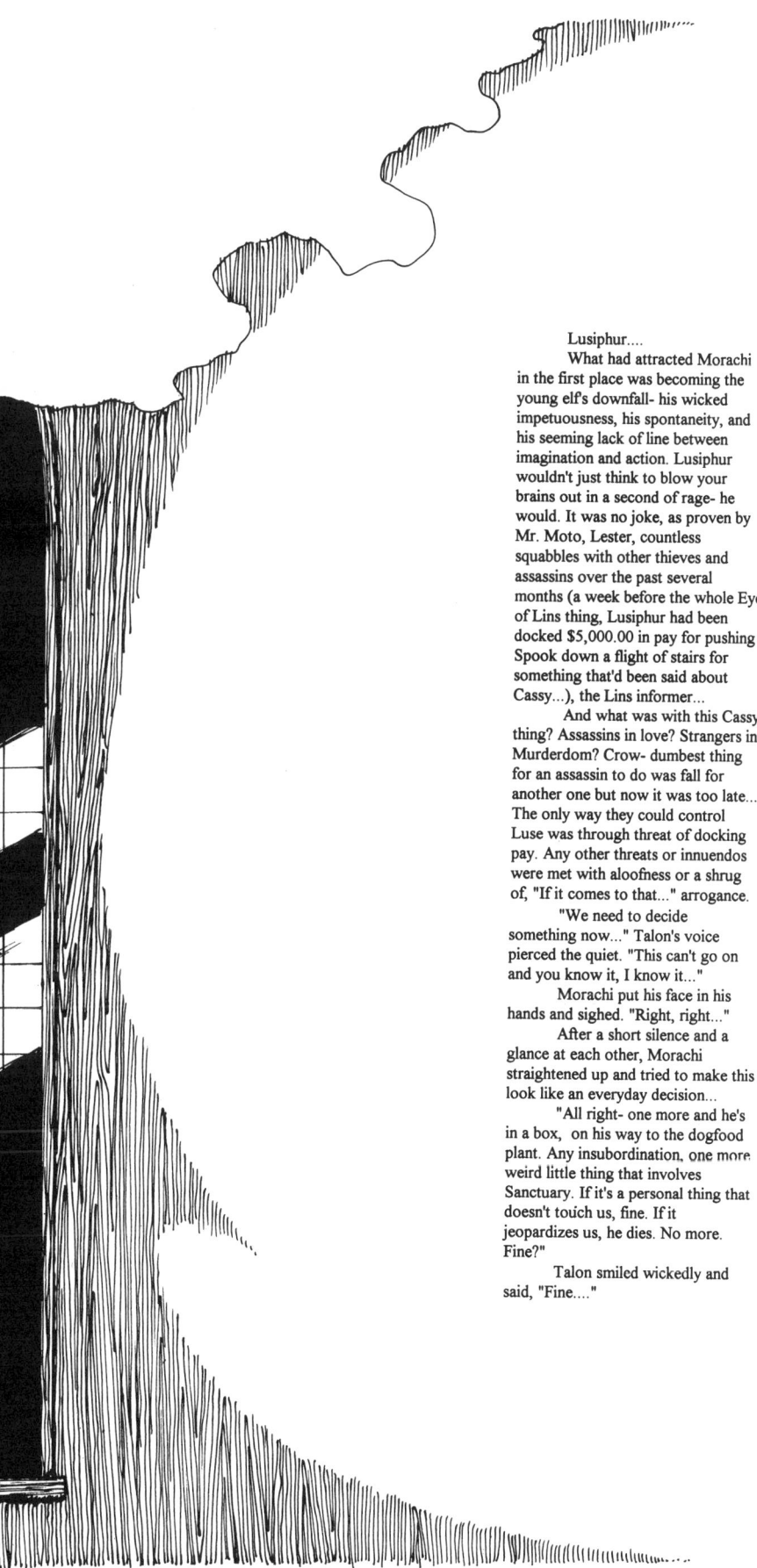

Lusiphur....

What had attracted Morachi in the first place was becoming the young elf's downfall- his wicked impetuousness, his spontaneity, and his seeming lack of line between imagination and action. Lusiphur wouldn't just think to blow your brains out in a second of rage- he would. It was no joke, as proven by Mr. Moto, Lester, countless squabbles with other thieves and assassins over the past several months (a week before the whole Eye of Lins thing, Lusiphur had been docked $5,000.00 in pay for pushing Spook down a flight of stairs for something that'd been said about Cassy...), the Lins informer...

And what was with this Cassy thing? Assassins in love? Strangers in Murderdom? Crow- dumbest thing for an assassin to do was fall for another one but now it was too late... The only way they could control Luse was through threat of docking pay. Any other threats or innuendos were met with aloofness or a shrug of, "If it comes to that..." arrogance.

"We need to decide something now..." Talon's voice pierced the quiet. "This can't go on and you know it, I know it..."

Morachi put his face in his hands and sighed. "Right, right..."

After a short silence and a glance at each other, Morachi straightened up and tried to make this look like an everyday decision...

"All right- one more and he's in a box, on his way to the dogfood plant. Any insubordination, one more weird little thing that involves Sanctuary. If it's a personal thing that doesn't touch us, fine. If it jeopardizes us, he dies. No more. Fine?"

Talon smiled wickedly and said, "Fine...."

THREE

THE TROUBLE TODAY WITH WOMEN

INEVITABLY...

I REALLY HOPE YOU DIDN'T PAY THESE GUYS IN CASH... REALLY...

I COULD HAVE GOTTEN YOU A COUPLE OF LEG-BREAKERS FROM THE SOUTHSIDE DIRT REAL CHEAP...

PLEASE...

YOU EXPECT I'D PAY FOR THE SERVICE OF TWO SUCH AS..?

"PLEASE" TO YOU, LUSIPHUR...

AND I'M GOING TO TRY VERY HARD FROM MAKING MY END OF THIS UNPLEASANT...

DON'T "KILL YOURSELF TRYING."

LOOK, HYENA, I'M NOT STUPID AND THIS GUTSY ACT IS MAKING ME SICK...

WHY THE HELL ARE YOU HERE..?

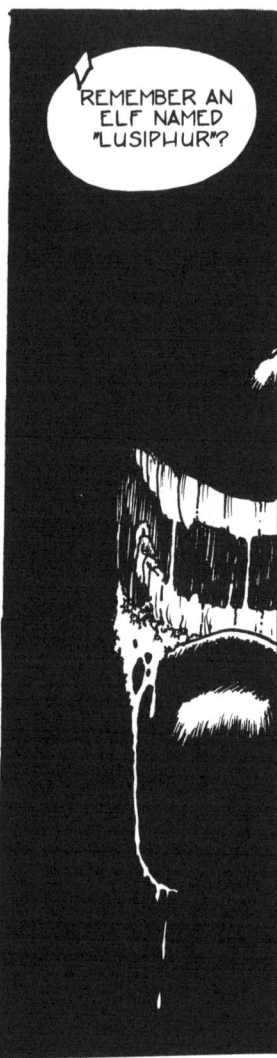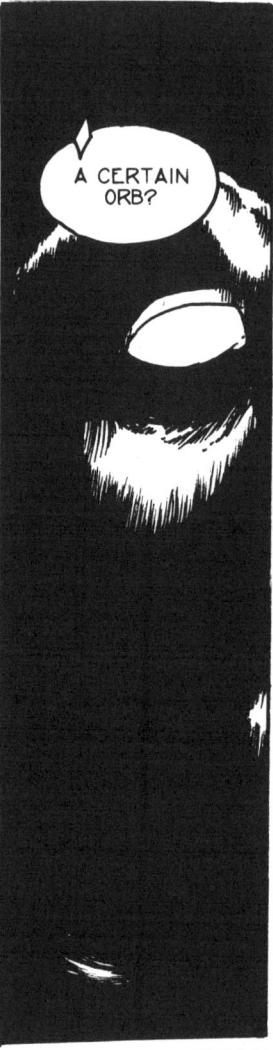

60

FOUR

F'IJA

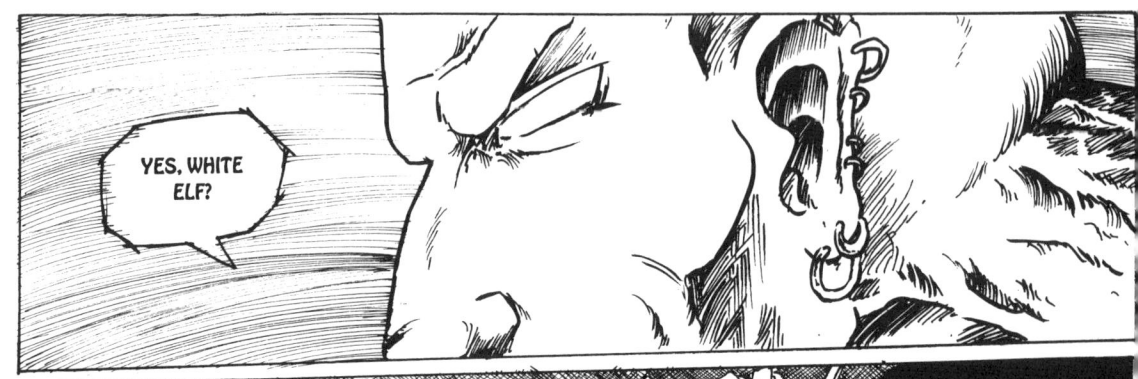

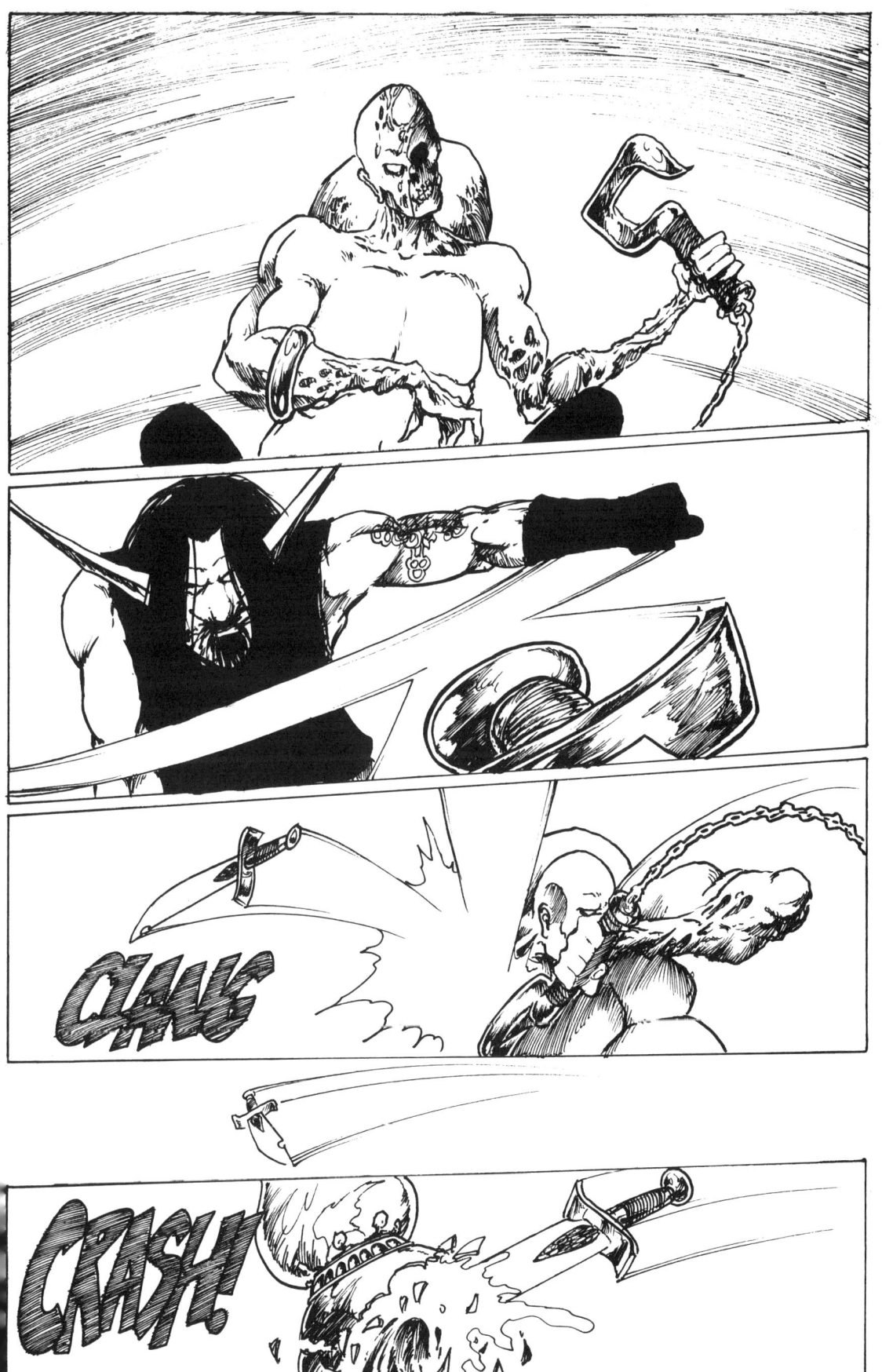

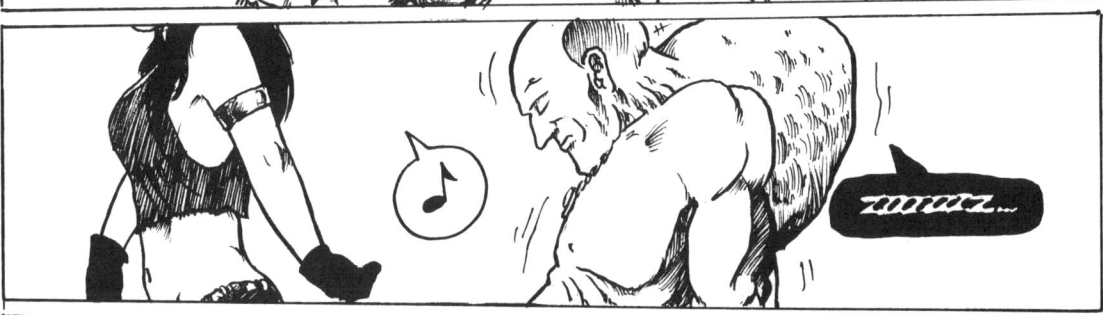

FIVE

WALKING SPANISH DOWN THE HALL

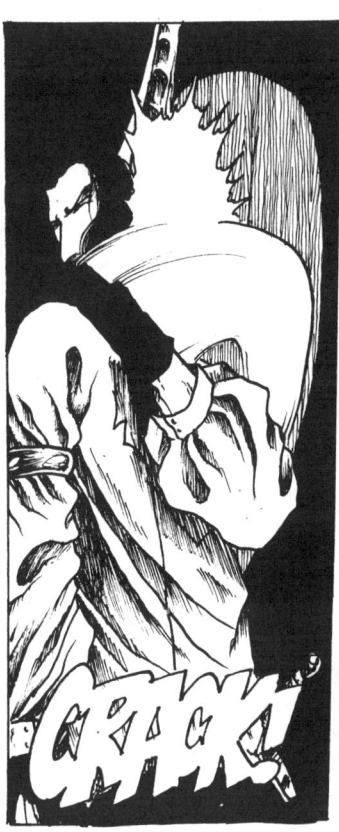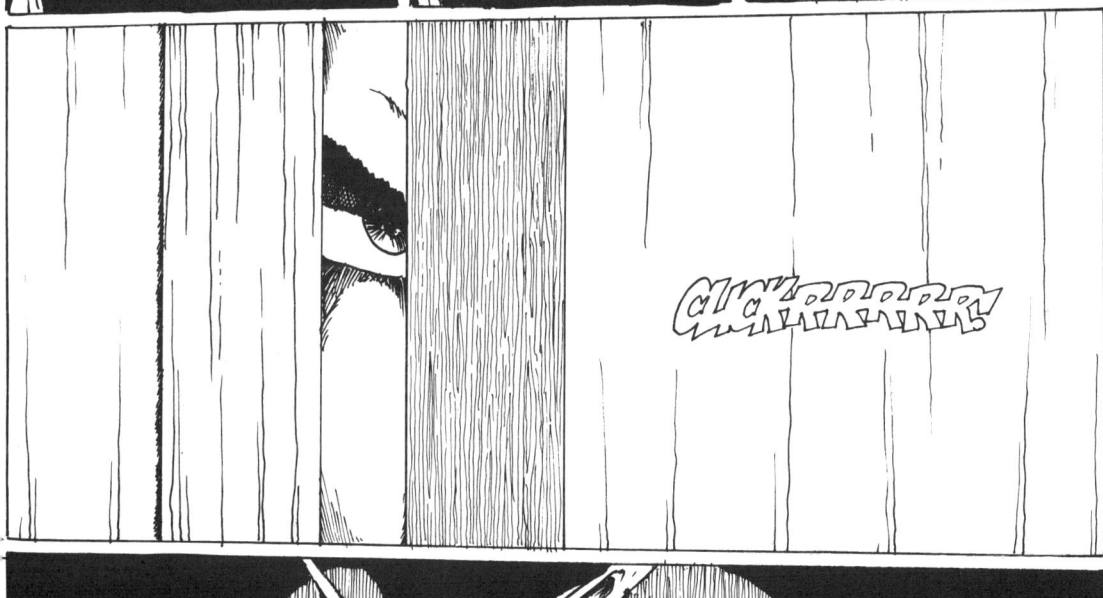

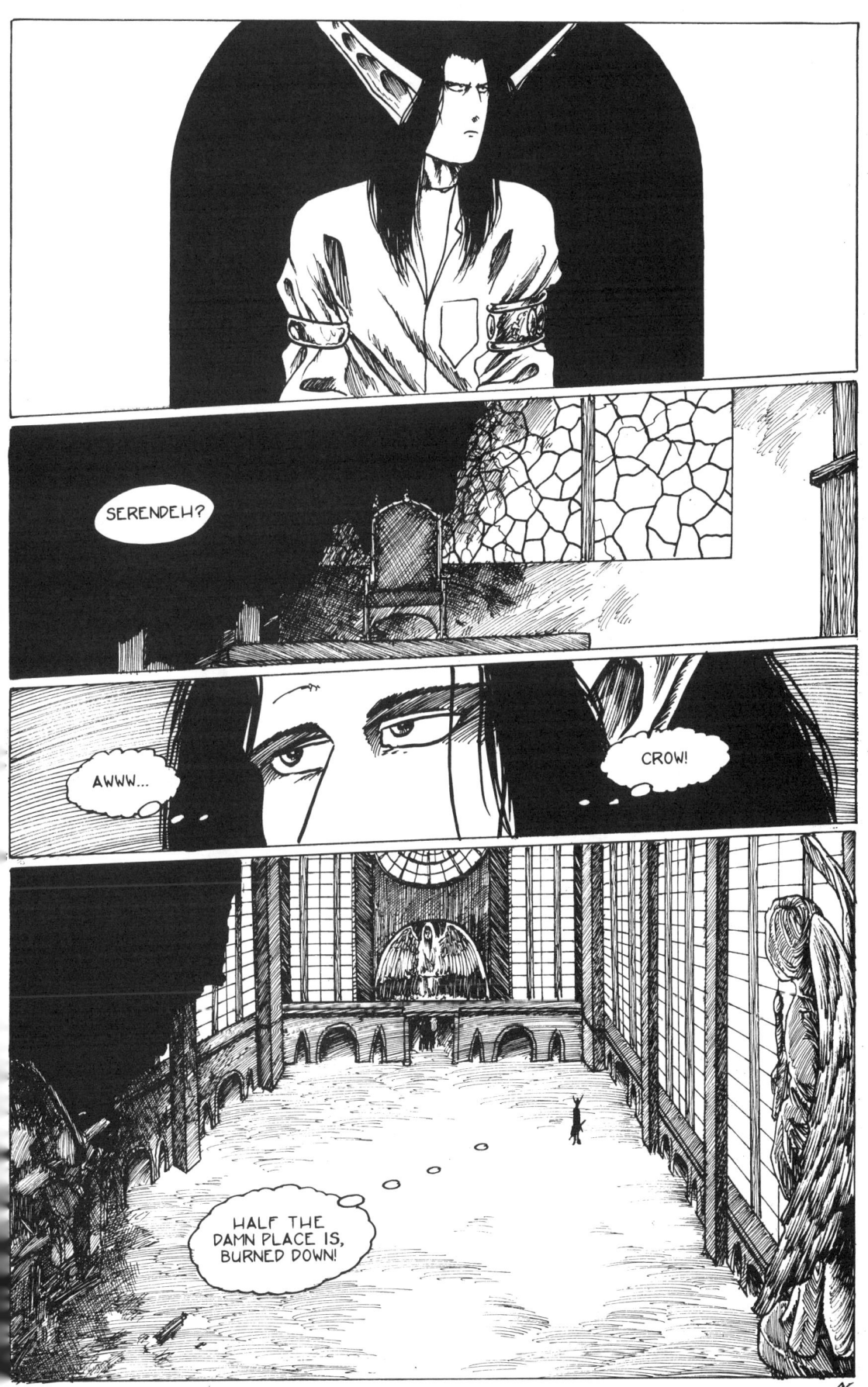

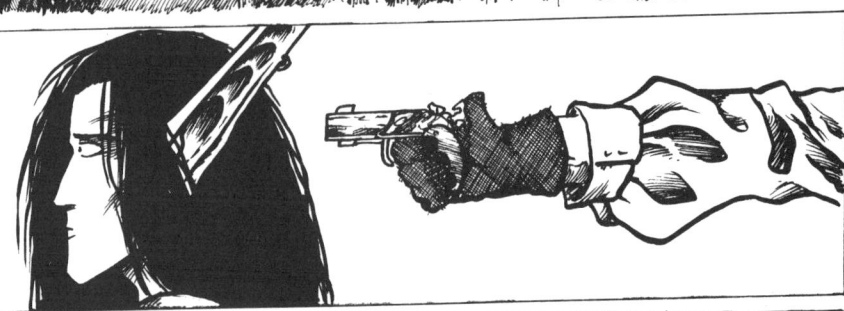

Thieves and assassins for ages have had their own underground code and laws. These are considered paramount to the discipline and status of the trait, and though are silent, unspoken, never written down, they are always accepted as an automatic incidental of the career choice. They are mandatory and unbreakable. For example, an assassin may never kill another assassin on what is considered neutral ground- places of Druidic worship, or any place or land designated sanctuary by a crime lord. To violate this rule would set every other assassin in organized or private employment after the individual who was foolhardy enough to break this, or any other, rule.

Private guilds of assassins and thieves had their own set of "sub- codes" that their members had to adhere to as well as these other given "Rules of Blood." Violation of these sub- codes was not considered blasphemy by the underground community but to the group employing said assassin/ thief, activities against these codes was considered always an act punishable by death. But whereas in the worldly code judgment was swift and usually unquestioned, Lords of the guilds found themselves in a predicament: if a guild leader took it upon himself to suffer death on the head of one of his own by his own mind and that only- the other killers and cutthroats had a tendency to lose respect for said Guildmaster. Therefore it was adopted long ago that there would be trials held for anyone in violation of Guild Law, totally separate from the Rules of Blood, unless the thieves or assassins trespasses led him into that territory as well.

Usually, though, in that case, the point of trial became moot.

This is what leads us to where we are. Lusiphur Amerellis Malache (or "Luse" for short) had been killing for the guild known as "Sanctuary" for approximately five months. It is now early May and the snows are melting in Mandratha, a northern city, largest metropolis in the west- Luse's hunting grounds.

Luse's tenure with the Sanctuary, run by the infamous brothers Morachi and Talon, two albino elves whom if you were to shake hands with, you'd best count your fingers walking away from, had been at best, shaky. Rapidly proving himself to be one of their best and coldest killers, as he'd done this sort of work in the past, he quickly earned their admiration. This, though, was short lived, as Lusiphur's personality (which is akin to a rattlesnake's temperament coupled with a mouth which delivers sarcasm faster than lightning hits the ground) and circumstance began to show them that Luse, while an excellent professional assassin, was also a risk to their organization.

So many things happened but in such a way that Lusiphur could not be directly singled out and punished for it without other members of the guild raising an eyebrow. This is something that no Guildmaster wants to deal with in any way. They must have the complete trust from their patrons that they are not the sort to go and "off" one of their own due to what is, in their perceptions alone, a crime or series of. This was mostly what the trials were for- to show a few of the more prominent guildmembers that they, the Lords, have far enough reason to merit out punishment to said individual. In this case, Lusiphur.

The trial went as such. The accused was given his or her choice in whom they wished to defend them. The Guildmaster(s) were the prosecution. The judge was usually the guild surgeon or Mage, were a guild lucky enough to have one. The charges were presented in chronological order and dealt with one by one. If the defendant was found innocent, he was let go of the service of the guild. If he/ she was found guilty, they were executed.

The trial was viewed by five witnesses, members of the guild, that they might go out and relate to the other members what had transpired. Usually this was found fair and peace remained unquestioned.

For his defender, Luse had chosen Fleece, a human assassin. He would have chosen Cassandra, his beloved, but she was out on a hit. The Judge in this case was an individual known as "The Judge," a real circuit judge who gave hits to Sanctuary- usually consisting of criminals who'd escaped his courtroom on some loophole in the written word of the law. It was on his assignment Cassy was out on now.

Sanctuary's healer had quit the day before the trial, and usually their Mage oversaw these hearings but for some reason known only to him had protested involvement in the trial of

Lusıphur. He did sit off to a corner, silently watching while concentrating his powers in keeping the Church locked in the nowhere dimension it resided in.

The room was small and ill lit. The Judge sat in his hooded robes behind a great oak desk, gavel in front of him, as well as a clay flagon of coffee, a writing pad and quill. Before him sat to the front left Morachi and Talon and to his front right, Fleece and the manacled Lusiphur.

Most of the time this was not considered necessary, but Lusiphur was a killer to the bone. Even with Morachi and Talon fully armed in the room, the assassin's things- swordbelt included sat not 15 feet away beside Serendeh, the Mage, and Luse was a rank murderer, armed or not. Best to play it safe here.

Five members of Sanctuary lined the wall. Spook, an assassin as well, was the only killer present as witness. The rest were thieves, who usually needed more story backing up anyway.

Lusiphur sat with a scowl on his face. He was aware of several things... It was keeping aware of his advantages that had kept him alive all these years. Right now, as the trial was soon to begin, he counted them...

When Fleece had searched him for weapons, he had not mentioned the gun strapped to the small of the Elf's back, nor the dagger in his boot. They, all of them, had overlooked the fact that he was wearing spurs and his ankles were not chained. He was still wearing his chainmail shirt under his black undershirt. Serendeh had, for some reason, abstained from standing as judge in this matter- which the Elf could only figure meant the Mage, for some reason, did not approve of these proceedings.

Well, neither did he. The rogue glared about the room, imagining all who fell under his eye suddenly exploding into little bloody chunks under the ferocity of his anger and hatred. He realized full and well why he was here, but reasoned, as usual Lusiphur fashion, himself a victim of poor circumstance. His mind screamed for a cigarette...

He leaned over to Fleece, "You have a cigarette?" Fleece, arms folded across his chest, leaned in and whispered, "Left 'em in my room... Sorry..."

"Some lawyer you..." Luse growled. His gaze fell on Morachi and Talon. "You boys got a cigarette?" He asked cheerfully.

The two brothers looked at eachother in amazement and back at Luse. "No." Said Talon flatly as Morachi just shook his head. Luse leaned back smiling bitterly. *Well,* he thought, *if they're going to insist on this fiasco then I'm certainly not going to make it pleasant for them...*

The Judge then cleared his throat, and, in an old, hiss- like voice, said, "You must all forgive me if this trial goes a bit awkwardly. I am not used to adjudicating for the underground. While I understand it's politics there is a little shadow on the exact process. But I do demand the same obedience and professionalism I am used to in a real courtroom. I will rule fairly and impartially, and if this young- er, Elf is guilty of that which he is accused of, I will have no inhibitions ruling so. I also as well, expect there to be no arguing if I happen to see things differently than the present Guildmasters, Morachi and Talon. The one issue I would like to discuss at this point is contempt of court...

"While there are certain punishments I can administer in the real world, there is no time nor place for them here. So to insure there is no extended bickering, or any commotion from the peanut gallery- whether that be the witnesses, the defendant, or the prosecution, I would like to, ummmm, invent a rule of this..."

Lusiphur noticed Morachi nod his head towards The Judge after a moment's thought. The old man continued, "Fine. I will usher three warnings. After that, the offender loses a finger."

Morachi blanched a moment and then nodded again.

He's thinking I'll crack first... Lusiphur thought angrily. *He's thinking, "Oh, that'll do cuz the little moron can't keep from cutting them up every second so by the midway here he'll be wiping his ass with his right foot!" Well I'll show him, the pasty faced... God, I really can't stop, can I...?*

"-the prosecution's arguments and charges,' The Judge was saying. "Morachi?"

Morachi, one of the tallest Elves Luse had ever seen, stood taking a lit cigar from his mouth and presented his case calmly coolly- just like he did everything else...

ONE

YOUR FUNERAL, MY TRIAL

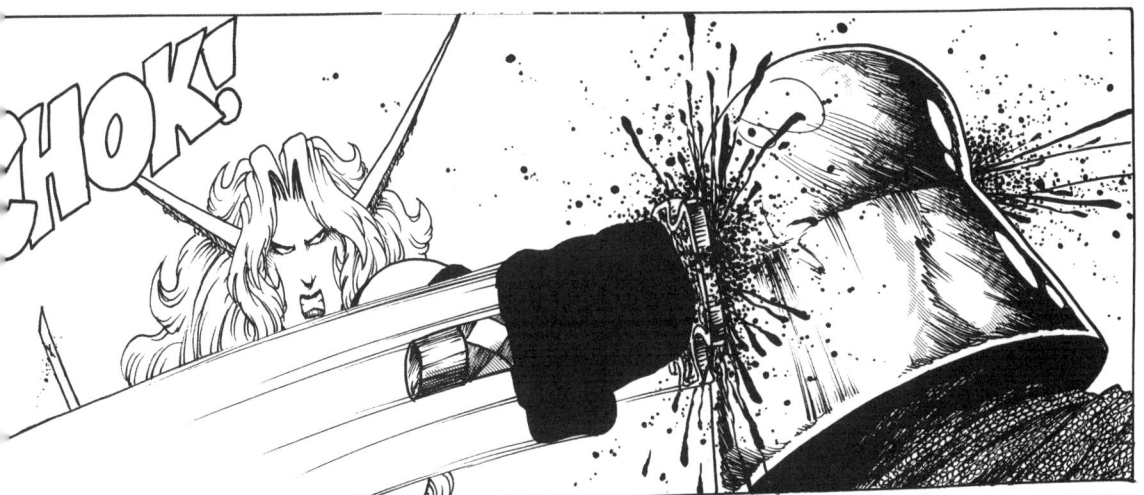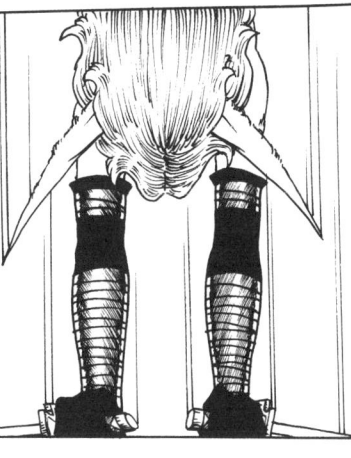

Jace chased Cassy hard through the wet streets and alleys of Mandratha. Cold air hissed in and out of his clenched teeth. He didn't know her name, who she was- only that she was an assassin for Sanctuary and that meant she probably knew where Lusiphur was. The more time had passed the more he somehow knew that getting word to his friend was critical, if not already too late. The Elf realized this might all be a game in his own mind but that made it his reality nonetheless, and that had been good enough for him the past three quarters of a century. It was with that judgment that he decided to quit the Elvin Army and to eventually come under the employment of Vido. His life of late had boiled down to trying to have as interesting a time as possible and as a means to do it, taking city guard positions. but these days even that didn't interest him. The short time he and Lusiphur wandered together-that was living. That was what life was for. Lusiphur's life seemed to center around abnormal circumstance, and that was what he lacked. Sometimes it seemed tragic, and sometimes hilarious- but never ever dull. It was almost something he envied, and would never regret being part of. And it seemed to him like things were long overdue at a point where the rogue needed someone to watch his back. That was why he had to catch this girl- to find his friend again...

GASP!

OH, LADY...

TRUST ME...

YOU REALLY DON'T WANT TO DO THAT...

"Your Honor, we, the Guildmasters of Sanctuary, bring charges up against the assassin Lusiphur... These charges are as follows...

"One, the murder of our trainer, Mr. Moto. Lusiphur was sent to him for assessment in his abilities shortly after joining Sanctuary and, in a three day period, managed to kill a long trusted associate of ours. the second charge is Lusiphur's involvement in the disappearance of the Lieutenant of Assassins, Lester, with whom Your Honor was familiar with. A day before Lester's disappearance, he'd returned from a hit, and Lusiphur, upon sight of him, attacked him with intent to kill. It was felt by talon and I that the best thing to do was to send Lester on a long range hit in order to allow Luse the time to cool off and accept his rival's presence in the guild. Lester left for his hit and has not been seen since. While Luse's whereabouts can be accounted for every hour between the attack and Lester's leaving, and there is no evidence that Lusiphur directly harmed in any way Lester in that time, we still view the circumstances of Lester's disappearance and their earlier display a bit too convenient for Lusiphur. We believe that somehow, Lusiphur managed to arrange it so that Lester could not return, and considering the place he was sent, this is tantamount to murdering Lester indirectly. Charge number three is the jeprodation of the guild's safety on many counts...

"First is his abduction by the Eye of the Lins, a rival guild trying to stake claim to Mandratha over Sanctuary. Lusiphur was interrogated by them and while told them nothing, in his escape brought a member back here-"

"Which enabled us to interrogate him and discover the location of their hide out!" Luse snarled defensively, half rising. The thought that Morachi could even bring this instance up in order to make him look bad infuriated the Elf. *That's it,* Lusiphur thought darkly.
He is now an enemy, and if I live for anything, it's to see those two pink- eyed bastards on their knees with their guts in their hands at my feet!

The Judge banged his gavel. "That was out of order! Another outburst like that will earn you a finger on my table... Continue, Morachi..."

Lusiphur settled back giving Fleece a cold look, thinking the Judge was going to get it worst of all once this was done and over. Hatred washed through every pore of his body, so he nearly shook with it. *Pig,* he thought blackly.

Morachi cleared his throat. "Yes, well, it jeprodized the guild nonetheless, despite what benefit may have come of it...

"Also, in the fight to bring the opposing guild down, Lusiphur killed a member of the Bloodgaurd- the police task force organized to find and destroy Sanctuary. Lusiphur had been told specifically upon his induction into Sanctuary that he was NEVER to harm in any way a member of police Lieutenant Vido's Bloodgaurd..."

Lusiphur, resisting mightily the urge to burst out again, leaned to Fleece and muttered in a voice shaking with rage, "I was told not to touch Vido, and Vido only, which I could have but did not! The slag I took was a sergeant or something- I never heard a word about that being wrong!" Fleece made a note of that and shushed Lusiphur, "Calm down, man. We'll get our say here soon..."

Luse sat back again, beginning to try to manipulate the manacles that bound his wrists.

"recently when an old score of Luse's came back," Morachi was saying. "A dimension jumping assassin known as an E'jja. These beings are from an undefinable plane of existence and normally sent on hits through black magickings. They are almost indestructible as there is only one way to kill them, each one having a different way of dying. One came here after Lusiphur over some unknown past dispute between the two and killed members of Sanctuary- many thieves and two of our assassins, aside from half the structure being burned down in the attempt to control this being..."

"We, Talon and myself, as Lords of Sanctuary, believe these crimes are more than sufficient reason to see the execution of Lusiphur as he has jeprodized the safety of this guild more than

once and has broken directly many of it's laws with full forethought and malice. We are emphatic about our position and the laws we are to represent, and hope to see enforced here this day..."

Morachi sat and there was a silent stir throughout the room. Lusiphur shifted in his seat. The Judge was scribbling notes and Fleece sat nervously awaiting his turn. Morachi and Talon whispered to eachother and looked very pleased with themselves. The witnesses sat almost froze, looking at Lusiphur like they were viewing the corpse of a stranger. Luse glared back at them.

The Judge then nodded towards Fleece, and the slender assassin rose and cleared his throat. "Ummm... Yeah... Okay... Well, first off, Mr. Moto was an old, old human, and his death during the assessment of Lusiphur could be easily looked at as unfortunate circumstance. At the time, Morachi nor Talon expressed a whole lot of grief over the loss of the old man and Luse was in no way reprimanded for it at the time, so the fact that they're brining it up now as a charge against him is pretty bogus..." Fleece reddened at his use of streetslang and looked at the Judge, "Sorry, Your Honor..." the Judge nodded in understanding. "Go on as best you will, young man..."

Fleece, encouraged, looked at Luse with a bit of a sparkle in his eye. "Alright, " he said, looking around the courtroom and centering on the Judge. "As for the second charge, all evidence my client had ANYTHING to do with the disappearance of Lester is PURELY circumstantial and should be totally disregarded! Whatever fate befell Lester was, while unfortunate folly, and is, unknown. All WE know is that he has not returned from his hit. Maybe he was killed by his mark, lost his ahnk that could bring him back here- any number of a multitude of things could have gone wrong and only ONE possibility out of MILLIONS has to do with Lusiphur!"

Damn straight! Lusiphur thought, squaring his shoulders boldly. *How in the hell can ANYONE know I screwed his ahnk up so bad he'd be lucky to hock it for a crown let alone get back here with it!?!?!?*

Fleece went on. "As for the third charge, as my client already interrupted proceedings to make clear, he brought the member of the Eye of the Lins here, WITH HIS LEGS CUT OFF AND HALF DEAD, to interrogate! How an almost dead, legless man could be considered a threat to a guild chock full of thieves and assassins is an absolute JOKE!" He waved his hands about enthusiastically now, punctuating his points and reeling in righteousness. Luse rolled his eyes a bit and shook his head, smiling a bit.

"He was NEVER EVER told that ALL of Vido's men were off limits to harm- ONLY VIDO HIMSELF! Again, after this instance he was not lectured or reprimanded in ANY WAY, until now, it gets brought as a charge against him!" He snarled in disgust at Morachi and Talon for a second- then, realizing that at the end of this, he would still be working for them, flustered a moment and cleared his throat.

"Ummm... Yeah. Okay... That E'jja thing- how can he have helped that? He even faced the thing himself and was nearly killed by it. We all have pasts, and sometimes they come back to haunt us- rarely do we escape them for long. Lusiphur did not purposely antagonize the E'jja into coming here, and it is unknown WHY it came here but to kill Luse. In which case, as an assassin in the employment of Sanctuary, Morachi and Talon are in a position of obligation to protect Luse and, in fact, they are feeding him to the wolves over it...

"So you see, Your Honor, Morachi and Talon are merely trying to justify personal vendettas against Lusiphur in the guise of charges that fall under a code we all adhere to- even Lusiphur- and that which he has NOT in ANY WAY broken- but by unusual and TOTALLY circumstantial goings- on have worked seemingly in their favor to dispose of him! I leave it to the wisdom and experience of the Court to see this for what it is and to rule accordingly...."

Fleece sat down satisfied, Morachi and Talon glaring at him. Lusiphur smiled and said, "Not bad. Not bad..."

The Judge made notes and murmured, "Ten minutes to think, and I'll render my decision to the Court..."

PAST TALES OF THE ELF

POISON ELVES
Requiem for an Elf
Volume 1
by Drew Hayes

Collects Poison Elves (a.k.a. I, Lusiphur) issues #1-6 originally published by Mulehide Graphics.

Volume 1 introduces the misanthropic elvin wanderer known as Lusiphur. In "Six-Tell Amlah," a nasty wizard cuts out Lusiphur's eye because he needs it to summon a demon of frightening power. In "Resurrection Man," Lusiphur finds himself the guest of a serial killer with an unhealthy attachment to his dead mother. In "Similitude of a Hero," Lusiphur runs into his arch enemy, the Purple Marauder, for the first time ever. In "Debt Collections," Lusiphur finds himself obliged to revisit his thieving days, with dire consequences.

$14.95 US - 144 pages   ISBN 1-57989-001-6

PAST TALES OF THE ELF

POISON ELVES

Traumatic Dogs
Volume 2
by Drew Hayes

Collects Poison Elves (a.k.a. I, Lusiphur) issues #7-12 originally published by Mulehide Graphics.

Volume 2 begins with "The Countess," wherein Lusiphur passes himself off as "Lord Wesley" and ends up in the clutches of the most disgusting Countess in all of Amrahly'nn. In "Wicked Yawn" (Drew's homage to Neil Gaiman), Lusiphur meets Parintachin, the demon that lives in his head. In "Night of the Doppelganger," Lusiphur fights an ancient beast whose shape-shifting power makes it nearly invincible. "Suicide Kings" is the tragic story of Siamese twins and the woman who didn't love either of them. "Sleeping in Mistwood" places Lusiphur back into the most disturbing environment in the Poison Elves universe: his own head. And finally, "Hyena" introduces Lusiphur's ex-wife, Hyena (hence the name of the story).

$14.95 US - 144 pages   ISBN 1-57989-002-4

PAST TALES OF THE ELF

POISON ELVES

Desert of the Third Sin

Volume 3
by Drew Hayes

Collects Poison Elves issues #13-18 originally published by Mulehide Graphics.

Volume 3 collects the entire "Desert of the Third Sin" saga, considered by many to be the best story-arc in the series' Mulehide run. It chronicles the three wishes granted to Lusiphur by a djinni, and the consequences Lusiphur must face as a result of the wishes he makes. First, he must fight Ailwon San Cennlach over the ownership of Cinlach, a magic elvin sword. This battle attracts the attention of Tenth, a mysterious elvin wizard who refuses to be left out of the action. Finally, Lusiphur faces the E'jja Widowmaker, who can only be killed by one method. Unfortunately, no one knows what that method is...

$14.95 US - 144 pages   ISBN 1-57989-003-2

PAST TALES OF THE ELF

POISON ELVES

Patrons

Volume 4
by
Drew Hayes

Collects Poison Elves issues #19-20

Originally published by Mulehide Graphics.

Reprinting #19-20 of Mulehide Graphic's Original Poison Elves Series

Volume 4 collects the last two issues in the Mulehide series. In "The Gypsy and the Troll," Lusiphur and his new traveling companion, Jace, save a damsel in distress from a dark troll, which is okay except that dark trolls were thought to be extinct. In "Lord of the Lilacs," the purple marauder makes a return appearance, just to annoy Lusiphur and cause him great emotional pain.

$4.95 US - 48 pages   ISBN 1-57989-017-2

PAST TALES OF THE ELF

Sanctuary

VOLUME 5
BY
DREW HAYES

COLLECTS
POISON ELVES
ISSUES #1-12
(FROM THE
SIRIUS SERIES).

Volume 5 tells the first half of the massive "Sanctuary" storyline, in which Lusiphur joins an assassin's guild in Mandratha, the largest city in Amrahly'nn. After passing their various test for membership, Lusiphur begins a stormy romance with fellow assassin Cassandra and butts heads with Lester, a sworn enemy from his past. Meanwhile, police Lieutenant Vido begins narrowing his search for the assassins of Mandratha while Lusiphur's old traveling companion, Jace, joins the Lieutenant in that search for reasons of his own...

$14.95 US - 272 pages   ISBN 1-57989-022-9

MISSING PART OF THE SAGA?
POISON ELVES
BY DREW HAYES

VOLUME 1
144pp.....$14.95

VOLUME 2
144pp.....$14.95

VOLUME 3
144pp.....$14.95

VOLUME 4
48pp.....$4.95

VOLUME 5
272pp.....$14.95

POSTER #1
22" x 34".....$5.95

COSMIC THERAPY
P.O. BOX 1309 ANDOVER, NJ 07821
(973) 328-6606

▲ Please add $5.00 for Shipping & Handling for first FIVE ITEMS.
▲ Add an additional $1.00 for each additional item (e.g. 5 items add the minimum $5.00, 7 items add $7.00)
▲ Orders outside the U.S.A. by Credit Card ONLY. Shipping will be billed at the exact rate at time of shipment. Please call or fax for more information.
▲ Allow 4-6 weeks for delivery. US Post or UPS at our discretion.
▲ SATISFACTION GUARANTEED. No refunds.
▲ Defective, damaged or incorrect orders may be returned for exchange or credit. Please call or write for authorization first. Have your Invoice # ready.
▲ Checks and money orders in US funds ONLY, payable to COSMIC THERAPY. Checks must clear prior to shipping. Returned checks will be charged $15.00. No COD'S.
▲ If you wish to pay by Visa or Mastercard you must send your: Card Number, Expiration Date, Authorizing Signature, Phone Number or call us at 973-328-6606.
▲ Wholesale inquires welcomed. Offer good while supplies last.

PE_TPB